Bristol Libraries

1800493463

The Enforcer
ANNA PERRIN

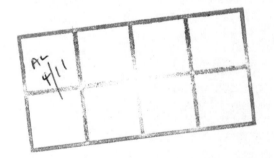

MILLS & BOON®

All the characters in this book have no existence outside
the imagination of the author, and have no relation
whatsoever to anyone bearing the same name or names.
They are not even distantly inspired by any individual
known or unknown to the author, and all the incidents
are pure invention.

All Rights Reserved including the right of reproduction
in whole or in part in any form. This edition is published
by arrangement with Harlequin Enterprises II BV/S.à.r.l.
The text of this publication or any part thereof may
not be reproduced or transmitted in any form or
by any means, electronic or mechanical, including
photocopying, recording, storage in an information
retrieval system, or otherwise, without the written
permission of the publisher.

® and TM are trademarks owned and used by the
trademark owner and/or its licensee. Trademarks marked
with ® are registered with the United Kingdom Patent
Office and/or the Office for Harmonisation in the
Internal Market and in other countries.

First published in Great Britain 2011
Large Print edition 2011
Harlequin Mills & Boon Limited,
Eton House, 18-24 Paradise Road,
Richmond, Surrey TW9 1SR

© Anna Perrin 2010

ISBN: 978 0 263 21786 5

Harlequin Mills & Boon policy is to use papers that
are natural, renewable and recyclable products and
made from wood grown in sustainable forests. The
logging and manufacturing process conform to the legal
environmental regulations of the country of origin.

Printed and bound in Great Britain
by CPI Antony Rowe, Chippenham, Wiltshire

ANNA PERRIN

grew up reading romance novels and thrillers so it's no surprise that she loves writing romantic suspense. A two-time finalist in the RWA Golden Heart contest, she is delighted by the publication of her first Intrigue. She avoids housework as much as possible and enjoys hanging out with her supportive husband, two terrific daughters and pets including a temperamental calico, a blue-eyed husky and a mixed-breed horse.

To Patience Smith,
who made my dream of publication
happen. Thank you.

To Brenda Harlen, who brainstorms
with me during dinners and road
trips. What an extraordinary CP and
friend. And to my wonderful family.
You mean everything to me.

Chapter One

"What do you mean, he's escaped?"

Dr. Claire Lamont gripped her cell phone tighter and stared out her kitchen window at the slashing rain. Two days ago, she had sent FBI agent Andy Forrester to Ridsdale Psychiatric Hospital for evaluation. *Now he was out?*

Gene Welland, her contact at the Bureau's Cincinnati office, said, "At eight o'clock Forrester was in his room, an hour later he was gone."

The explanation didn't make sense to her.

Not with the state-of-the-art security measures at the facility. "How could that happen?"

"We think he had inside help."

"You suspect Ridsdale staff?" she asked, pacing between the wall oven and the granite-topped island. "Or someone within the Bureau?"

"Too soon to point a finger," Gene said, clearly in no mood to speculate. "I'm calling because a nurse at the hospital reported he threatened to kill you."

Dread twisted in her stomach. Her gaze darted to the patio door. One forceful blow would smash the glass, then Forrester could slip a hand inside, twist the lock and—

She stopped pacing. Exhaled a deep breath. A long day of interviews and flight delays had set her on edge. "Forrester probably lashed out at me without meaning it."

Or maybe he did mean it. Maybe he was

in such a rage about her confining him to Ridsdale that he'd try to harm her.

She resumed pacing, her mouth dry, her palms sweating. Thunder rumbled in the distance and a streak of lightning sliced through the sky.

"I'm not taking any chances," Gene said. "In fact, I've already sent an agent to pick you up, so get ready to leave."

"I'm just back from Minneapolis. My luggage is still in my front hall."

"Then you'll be set to go when our guy gets there."

What if her enraged patient showed up first?

"I have a better idea," she said. "You know the coffee shop where we met last month?"

"Java Heaven?"

"That's it. I'll meet him there."

After a short silence, Gene relented. "Okay,

Lisa is calling Brent to redirect him to that location."

Brent? As in Brent don't-waste-my-time Young?

Please let there be another agent in the Cincinnati office with the same first name.

"Who are we talking about?" she asked.

"Brent Young."

Damn. That was the field agent she'd met several weeks earlier when Gene had asked her to talk to his team after the shooting death of a colleague, Pete Sanderson. No degree in psychology was necessary to interpret Young's slouched posture, guarded expression or impatient tapping of his foot. Obviously, he viewed her presentation about counseling options as useless and had only shown up because he'd been ordered to.

Young's disdain for counseling hadn't surprised her. What *had* surprised her was the surge of attraction she'd felt for him. With his linebacker shoulders, coal-black hair and cheekbones that hinted at a Native American ancestor, he looked like a hard-core renegade. But there had been something appealing about his smile—which he'd let loose a few times in response to his colleagues' wisecracks. Against all logic, she wished *her* remarks had elicited the same response.

The wind rattled the panes of glass. The storm was getting worse.

"You can count on Brent to protect you," Gene said, correctly interpreting her silence as a lack of enthusiasm for her escort.

The overhead light went out, plunging the room into darkness. "Oh no," she muttered.

"What's wrong?"

"The storm just killed the power." She lifted her free hand, but she couldn't see it—or anything else.

"Check outside," Gene said, his tone urgent. "See if the streetlights are on."

Hadn't he been listening to her? No power meant no streetlights. Unless—

Understanding dawned on her, followed by a stab of fear. *Unless somebody had cut the power to her house.*

Still holding her cell phone, she rushed to the window. After what seemed like an eternity, her shaking fingers forced apart two slats of the horizontal blinds.

"The whole neighborhood's dark," she said, relief making her voice thin and breathless.

"Go to Java Heaven. Call me when you get there."

Pocketing her phone, she stared into the surrounding darkness. Collecting her luggage and shoes would be a lot easier if she had even a glimmer of light. She headed into the hall, where she kept a flashlight in a maple cabinet.

As her outstretched hands made contact with the wood, the basement stairs creaked. She froze, listening for more creaks. The only sounds were the ones made by the storm driving rain against the windows and the pounding of her heart.

She retrieved the flashlight, walked two steps. Stopped and listened again. Nothing.

The knotted muscles in her shoulders relaxed, and she nearly laughed. Gene's call had made her jumpy. She was alone in her home. Of course, she was alone.

No creak this time. A soft rustle. The shifting of clothes. *Someone was in the hall.*

Fear shot through her. She bolted for the front door.

When a deep baritone ordered, "Stop," she whirled around and smashed the flashlight into the source of that voice.

His surprised yelp was extremely satisfying. She swung the flashlight again but didn't connect this time. Instead, a muscled forearm shoved her backward. She fell hard against the wall, crying out as her right shoulder absorbed the brunt of the impact.

The flashlight bumped against the door frame.

Oh God, let the batteries work.

She depressed the switch. A brilliant beam erupted from the cylinder, and she directed it at his face, hoping to blind him. But the circle of light revealed he had his head tipped back and his hand over his nose. Blood streamed down his clean-shaven face.

Forrester had a beard.

"Nice work, doc. You damn near broke my nose."

Anxiety must have dulled her senses earlier because this time she recognized his voice. The man dripping blood all over her front hall was Brent Young, not the mentally unstable agent who'd threatened her.

She sagged against the wall in relief.

"Don't you dare faint on me," he said. "If anybody deserves to pass out, it's me. I got knifed by a junkie last year, and it didn't bleed this much."

If Young expected an apology, he'd be disappointed. She had nearly suffered a heart attack because of him. "You were supposed to meet me at Java Heaven. Didn't Gene's assistant call you?"

He looked at her, his eyes narrowed against the glare of the flashlight. "My cell vibrated, but I was too busy to answer it—"

"—because you were breaking into my house, right?"

He gripped her wrist, redirecting the beam of light toward the floor. "I arrived just before you did and wanted to make sure Forrester wasn't hiding inside. By the way, you should have bars installed on your basement windows."

"I'll add it to my chore list," she muttered.

His next words were barely more than a whisper. "Aren't you glad it's me, not Forrester, here with you now?"

In the semidarkness, his voice sounded intimate, seductive. Warmth from his hand seeped through her skin and traveled up her arm. Her heart beat faster, but this time fear wasn't the cause. It was attraction, raw and potent. An attraction that roared through her blood, demanding release. An attraction she had to suppress.

She jerked her wrist out of his grasp.

He gave a low, knowing chuckle.

Gene respected Young's ability to keep her safe. She shouldn't let him unsettle her.

"Let's head out," he said.

"I need my shoes."

He nodded, then cursed softly. The movement must have started his nose bleeding again. She thought of offering him ice, but it seemed prudent to leave immediately. They could stop and buy ice when they were well away from here.

She shone the flashlight around the hall. The beam illuminated her sneakers in the corner, and she shoved her feet into them. Then she aimed the flashlight toward the spot where she'd left her luggage.

A noise like a car backfiring sounded outside. In the same instant, the pane of glass beside the front door shattered, and a tiny round hole appeared on the side of her carry-on case.

Her blood turned cold.

The bullet had missed her by inches.

BRENT CURSED as a second bullet plowed into the case. The flashlight was a beacon for the bastard outside.

He knocked the traitorous item out of Claire's hand, dragged her to the floor and covered her with his body. Her full breasts rose and fell in agitation. Under other circumstances, he would have enjoyed the softness of those curves, but tonight wasn't about pleasure. It was about staying alive.

The shooting stopped—probably because the flashlight had gone out after hitting the floor. But the threat wasn't over. Whoever was out there couldn't know if he'd hit his target unless he ventured inside.

Brent placed his lips against her ear and murmured, "Let's go."

"Which way?" she whispered back.

"Back door. Stay low. No noise."

"You need to move if you expect me to."

She shifted, her pelvis bumped against his, reminding him that it had been months since he'd been this close to a woman. Maybe after the danger was over, he'd think about remedying that situation—but not with her.

She wasn't unattractive. Far from it. He didn't remember a word of her info session, but he sure remembered *her*. Dark blond hair, full lips, flawless skin and a dynamite figure that even a tailored navy suit couldn't conceal. Claire Lamont had definite assets, but she was also a shrink. In his experience, shrinks were trouble, and he'd be a fool to forget it now just because this one came with a husky voice and a curvy body.

Cool, damp air flooded in through the broken glass pane. He climbed to his feet and crept along the hall. The back door was situated off the laundry room. When he reached it, Claire was right behind him.

"Now what?" she asked.

"Wait here."

He felt his way through the dark to the connecting door to the garage. Because of the power failure, he couldn't hit the switch to open the garage door. The automatic opener had to be disconnected from the overhead framework so he could lift the door manually.

He descended the wooden steps into the garage. A moment later, his leg nudged the bumper of Claire's car. He skirted around the driver's side and went to stand behind the vehicle. Should be a rope dangling with a handle attached. Reaching up, he moved his hand back and forth, trying to locate it.

Nothing.

Growing impatient, he climbed onto the trunk. The added height made it possible for him to touch the mechanism directly. He reached out, then inhaled as a sharp metal edge nicked his thumb. Damn. This fumbling around in the dark was crazy, but he couldn't risk using the penlight in his pocket. The garage had windows facing onto the front walkway.

Several tries later, he released the hook from the frame. He slid off the car and reached for the garage door. Twisting the handle, he tugged hard. The garage door rolled upward with a loud screech. Hopefully, the shooter would think Claire was attempting to drive away and try to stop her.

He ran back to the connecting door, knowing that it wouldn't take the shooter long to search the garage. He'd likely shoot the lock off the inner door and head inside.

Brent crossed the laundry room to the back door, stretched out both hands, but encountered only empty space.

"Claire?" he whispered.

No response. *Damn this darkness.*

Retrieving the penlight from his pocket, he shone it around him. The sliver of light flickered over the confined space, revealing a washer, dryer, sink and three-foot-long counter for folding clothes. And nothing else. His frustration surged to a new level. Where the hell had she gone?

Turning on his heel, he aimed the penlight toward the hall. The narrow beam illuminated her suitcase with its two ugly bullet holes. An equally ugly thought crossed his mind. What if Claire hadn't left the laundry room voluntarily? The possibility choked off his annoyance like a tourniquet, and alarm took its place. He'd only spent two or three minutes in the garage, but that could have been enough time for Claire to be dragged out the back door and forced into a waiting vehicle.

A quiet click sounded. The back of his neck prickled.

He removed his semiautomatic pistol from its holster and headed into the hall. As he drew near the kitchen, the pantry door swung open. He aimed his weapon. Despite the cold air seeping in through the broken window, sweat broke out on his brow.

When Claire emerged alone, his relief quickly gave way to anger. "Why didn't you wait for me in the laundry room?"

"Nowhere to hide if the guy broke in before you came back."

A reasonable explanation, but he wasn't about to admit it. "You just took ten years off my life."

"Then I guess we're even."

He knew he'd terrified her earlier. Not his intention, but before he could explain his presence, she'd walloped him in the face with the flashlight. After that, he'd lost all interest in apologizing.

"Come on," he said, turning away.

When he reached the back door, he stopped. "I'll go out first. If it's safe, I'll whistle. Run to the hedge on the right, wait for my next signal, then cross into your neighbor's yard. This time, stick to the plan."

"I will," she promised.

Something settled on the floor beside her. "What's that?"

"My carry-on."

"Leave it. It'll slow you down."

"No, it won't."

He decided to try a different tack. "Look, we'll stop at a store later, and you can pick up whatever you need."

"Thanks, but what I need is in this bag."

He couldn't believe they were arguing over toiletries. "Claire—"

"Save your breath," she told him. "I'm not going anywhere without it."

FORTUNATELY, YOUNG seemed to accept that arguing with her further would be a waste of time. Time they didn't have.

He headed out the back door, and she waited for his all-clear signal. He must think she was absurdly possessive. But if she divulged her reason for hanging on to her case—because it contained cassette tapes of her sessions with Forrester—Young might demand to listen to them later. And although Forrester had forfeited his right to patient confidentiality the instant he'd revealed his violent intentions, it was up to her to decide what information to share and what to withhold.

Young's signal came. She set off.

Freezing cold rain pelted her as she sprinted across the lawn to the hedge. In seconds, her jeans were plastered to her body like a wet second skin. She crouched low, her muscles tense with fear, knowing at any moment a bullet could slam into her. In the darkness, another of Young's low whistles sounded. Remembering his instructions, she followed him into her neighbors' yard. Unfortunately, their dog was outside, and his barking and snarling pinpointed their location with the same intensity as a siren.

"Run!" Young hollered.

She stretched out her legs and raced after him. The wet grass was slippery, but she managed to stay on her feet, pumping her arms to propel herself faster. Across the yard, down the street and around the corner. The speedy pace soon had her gasping for breath, but Young, running beside her, wasn't even winded, damn him. When she stumbled over a curb, he grabbed her arm.

"Keep going," he urged. "My car isn't far off."

A few minutes later, they reached a black Mustang.

"W-where are we going?" she asked, as they rocketed out of her neighborhood.

He didn't answer. He was too busy checking the rearview mirror. When he seemed satisfied that no one was following them, she repeated her question.

"I have a cabin on Camel Lake," he said. "Gene thought you'd be safest there."

She had heard of Camel Lake, but never been there. About a ninety-minute drive from Cincinnati, the lake was known for its clean water and excellent fishing. Gene must really be concerned about a breach of security if he didn't want her staying at one of the Bureau's safe houses in the city.

Rain dripped off the ends of her hair and trickled inside the scoop neck of her tank top. She was cold and uncomfortable. But her soaked clothes were only partly responsible for her discomfort. Young's presence accounted for the rest of it.

She glanced sideways at him. The glow from

the dashboard lit up his rugged profile and broad shoulders. All that maleness was unnerving, distracting. How long would she have to stay at the cabin with him?

Another rivulet of water streaked between her breasts. She shivered.

He cranked the heat up to its maximum setting. "There's a sweatshirt inside my gym bag," he said, motioning with his thumb toward the back of the car. "Help yourself."

She glanced over her shoulder at the bag. No way could she reach it without leaning over and sticking her backside up in the air.

"I'm okay," she said, even though her fingers were so chilled, she had to rub them to restore circulation.

"I promise it's clean."

His voice was low and persuasive, the same seductive tone she imagined he would use in bed. She rubbed her hands harder, berating herself for the wayward thought.

"I'll warn you," he said. "This heater takes forever to get hot."

He wasn't shivering at all. Maybe he was too hot-blooded to feel the cold. It certainly wasn't because he carried excess body fat. The sinewy arms and chest pressed against her body earlier were solid muscle.

"Claire?"

She was supposed to be considering his sweatshirt offer, not his physical attributes. And although she was tempted, she'd have to pass—on both. Donning clothes he had worn seemed so personal. She cleared her throat. "No, thanks."

He gave her a long, silent look, then returned his attention to the road.

Claire settled back and tried to assimilate

what had happened to her…and what had nearly happened.

Damn, that job offer in Minneapolis was looking good. No more one-on-one therapy sessions with traumatized patients. No more decisions about who was fit to return to work and who should go on disability. And, of course, no more heart-stopping incidents like tonight. Just twenty hours a week of teaching stress management techniques to executives.

"Gene said you had Forrester committed to Ridsdale for seventy-two-hour lockdown."

Abandoning her thoughts, she replied, "That's right."

"Why?"

Young's question surprised her. But maybe Gene had been too rushed for explanations. "During our last session, I uncovered his intention to kill someone."

"Who?"

"I don't know. The fire alarm went off, and we had to evacuate the building. Afterward, he wouldn't come back and continue our session. Sending him to Ridsdale was the only way I could ensure he wouldn't hurt anyone."

"Forrester definitely needs his head examined if he thinks shooting you is a smart move."

Shooting you.

The image of her own bleeding, bullet-riddled body made her shudder.

Had Forrester intended to kill her?

She wished she could believe he'd only wanted to scare her, but the shots had hit too close. A few inches to the right, and she would have died without ever seeing her executioner.

Without ever seeing...

She turned toward Young. "Did you see him tonight?"

"What?"

"When you left me, did you see Forrester?"

"No," he admitted.

"Then how can you be sure he shot at us?"

"You're the one who fingered him as a potential threat," Young said, irritation plain in his voice.

"What if it wasn't him?" Forrester might be the obvious candidate, but they lacked proof of his guilt.

"You lock up anybody else recently?"

She stiffened. "Of course not." Did he think she enjoyed confining patients to Ridsdale? That she got a kick out of exerting her power? Obviously, he didn't know her. An important point to remember the next time she felt the slightest twinge of attraction for him.

"Make somebody angry enough to want to see you dead?" he asked.

Her own anger made it hard to respond in a calm tone. "Not that I know of."

Young stabbed the dashboard with his forefinger. "Forrester had motive and opportunity. That makes him the prime suspect."

When she drew breath to respond, Young interjected, "Don't make this complicated, Dr. Lamont."

Folding her arms over her chest, she stared out the window. Young had made up his mind about Forrester. And although his arguments had merit, so did hers. He was just too stubborn to consider them.

The swishing sounds of tires on wet road and the clacking of the windshield wipers made the trip seem endless. After a while the rain stopped, and Young shut off the wipers. But the tension inside the Mustang didn't diminish.

Thirty minutes later, she spied a sign indicating Camel Lake on the right.

Young made the turn. "Almost there."

Several miles farther, the road became a narrow laneway.

Finally, he stopped the Mustang in a small clearing. Flicking on the overhead light, he dug through the glove compartment. She heard the jingle of keys, then the murmur of his deep voice. "I'm not sure what you're expecting, but the cabin's pretty rustic."

Rustic. A term used to make primitive dwellings sound charming.

She peered through the window at the surrounding darkness but couldn't detect anything that looked remotely man-made. With a sense of misgiving, she turned to him. "How rustic?"

He shrugged. "Basic amenities only."

"'Basic' includes indoor plumbing, right?" She wasn't expecting a complimentary robe, but the possibility of a dilapidated shack and outhouse had her wishing she'd asked for details earlier. Then again, it wasn't as if she'd had a lot of options.

He hesitated long enough to make her nervous before the corner of his mouth kicked up. "Yeah, there's plumbing."

That smile was the one she remembered from their first meeting, the one she had found so appealing, the one she had wanted to make happen. Now that she'd succeeded, she grew wary. Young's smile made him far too sexy.

Careful what you wish for.

Grabbing her carry-on, she exited the car. Young hustled around to the trunk, retrieved his gear and set off along a narrow, winding path through the woods.

A pale sliver of moon glowed in the sky, lending just enough light for them to walk without tripping over rocks and tree roots. Their footfalls made rustling noises in the grass. Other sounds carried on the night air. Water lapped against the shore. Crickets chirped noisily. An owl hooted in the distance. Normally, being surrounded by nature calmed her nerves, but tonight she was on edge. Of course, adrenaline could still be coursing through her blood from being shot at. That explanation was certainly less perturbing than the other possibility: sexual awareness of her companion.

She walked faster, telling herself she wasn't running away, she was merely anxious to reach her temporary accommodations.

A wooden structure appeared at the end of the path, nestled among the trees. Built entirely from rough-hewn logs, the cabin was larger than she had envisioned.

"How many bedrooms are there?" she asked, as Young climbed the porch steps.

"Two."

The right answer, since it meant neither of them would be stuck sleeping on the couch.

He unlocked the front door and stood aside so she could enter. She stepped over the threshold, more than a little curious to see the cabin's interior. With Young's guidance, she located the light switches. On the left side was a country-style kitchen. To the right, the main room contained a leather couch and several oversize chairs grouped in front of a granite fireplace. Floor-to-ceiling windows stretched the full length of one wall.

A flash of metal caught her eye. A silver trophy stood on the coffee table. She moved closer. What did Young excel at—besides making her uncomfortable?

The nameplate read 2007 Weir Marina Bass Derby Winners—Brent Young and Pete Sanderson.

Sanderson?

That was the name of the FBI colleague who had been shot—and evidently had been a close friend of Young. No wonder he had fidgeted throughout her presentation.

She edged away from the trophy, then shot him a glance. How was he taking it? Had the reality of his loss sunk in yet? Did he forget sometimes that his friend was dead? She didn't know him well enough to hazard a guess.

"The cabin hasn't been used since the fall," Young said.

She looked at the living room again, this time noting signs of neglect. Cobwebs clung to the central light fixture and a layer of dust coated every visible surface. Her nose registered the staleness of a place that hadn't been aired out in months.

"I guess you can't fish here in the winter," she commented.

His gaze fell on the trophy. "Sanderson convinced me to go ice-fishing in Alaska once. We just about froze solid…." For a brief, unguarded moment, Young's lips trembled and he squeezed his eyes shut.

Her heart twisted as she witnessed his struggle for composure. One thing she'd learned early in life: healing from grief was a painful process that often unfolded over years. This place had to hold so many memories. Would Young have come here now, if not for her need for a safe haven? His action displayed an inner strength that she couldn't help but admire.

"I'm sorry," she whispered, her throat so tight she could barely speak. "I'm sorry that your friend died."

Opening his eyes, Young pinned her with a furious glare. "Pete Sanderson didn't die. He was murdered. And when his killer is apprehended, he's the one who will be sorry."

His glare discouraged conversation, but she had to ask. "Do you know who killed him?"

He shook his head. "Fifteen agents are

assigned to the case. They've interviewed everyone known to have come in contact with him in the past two months. His recent assignments are also being reviewed for possible suspects."

So clinical. So emotionless. As if he were speaking about a stranger.

Everybody had different coping mechanisms. Apparently, Young's was to distance himself.

"With that many men assigned to the case, there'll be a break soon," she said.

A muscle in his jaw flexed. "No matter how long it takes, the bastard responsible for ending Sanderson's life *will* be brought to justice. I'm going to make sure of that."

Chapter Two

Brent grabbed the can of Folgers fine grind from the freezer, tossed half a dozen scoops into the coffeemaker and punched the on switch.

Why had he talked to Claire about Sanderson last night? That wasn't his way. In fact, he was known around the Bureau for being tight-lipped. Nobody knew anything about him outside of work. And even though his reticence had fueled wild speculation at times—especially regarding his choice of female companionship—he valued his privacy too much to divulge details of his personal life to anybody.

The only exception had been Pete. That man had known him inside out. His strengths, weaknesses, accomplishments and failures. And now his mentor—and best friend—was gone. Blown away in an abandoned warehouse two weeks ago.

The lack of progress in the investigation was gnawing at him. A prime suspect should have been identified by now. All those agents on the team and what had they come up with? Squat.

But it was more than frustration he'd felt last night. Returning to the cabin had hurt like hell. He'd never been here without Sanderson. For years, the two of them had deserted the city as often as they could. To fish and swim, drink beer and unwind from the pressures of work. Now the place was his. But everything about it—every stick of furniture, every fishing magazine, every boating knickknack—was a cruel reminder that those good times were gone forever.

Claire had picked up on that as soon as she'd seen the inscription on the trophy. The sympathy in her eyes had drawn him in, dulled the memories, eased his pain a little….

He'd quickly reminded himself that she'd been trained to show concern in these types of situations. Just as she'd been trained to dig around inside people's psyches, ferret out their innermost secrets and then slap labels on them.

Oh, yeah. He knew from bitter experience more than he wanted to about psychologists and their modus operandi.

Safeguarding an FBI shrink was the last assignment he'd have ever chosen. But it wasn't up to him to choose. Guys like Gene Welland made those calls. His role was to fulfill the requirements of the job with kick-ass proficiency. Protecting Claire would be no exception. Even though he couldn't respect her profession, he would watch over her as though she were the most important person in the world.

He'd just have to take care he didn't let his feelings about Sanderson surface again.

CLAIRE REACHED for her carry-on as soon as she awoke the next morning, eager to listen to the tapes of her sessions with Forrester. Fortunately, it was her standard practice, with the consent of her patients, to tape all her appointments. It saved her breaking eye contact to make notes. It also resulted in a more accurate record of the topics she and her patients discussed.

She had packed the tapes for her trip to Minneapolis, hoping to review them there, but there had been no time. The CEO of Balanced Life Consulting Group had kept her occupied with meetings, then made her a very generous offer which she had not yet accepted. There was so much to consider. Such as, was she ready to admit defeat and quit the Bureau? More than pride was at stake. She'd also be betraying the promise she'd made to herself at her father's graveside.

She couldn't dwell on that now.

Last night she'd been too strung out to tackle the tapes. But with Forrester no longer confined to Ridsdale, she needed to gain a better understanding of the man and his intentions. To do that, she would search her recordings for subtle nuances, crucial words she'd missed before, anything that would identify his intended victim.

She retrieved the tape recorder from the center section of the carry-on, then turned the bag over. A bullet had pierced the outside pocket. She dug inside, her heart pounding. Only one of the three tapes had survived undamaged. She peered at the label, breathing a sigh of relief when she saw the tape was of their latest session, the one she considered to be the most critical.

Sitting cross-legged on the bed, she inserted the tape, then put on the headphones and hit the play button.

She heard herself say, "You seem very agitated today, Andy. Do you want to tell me why?"

There was a noticeable pause on the tape.

"Did something happen?" she prodded.

After a while, he muttered, "Should have been a perfect MIOG op. Instead, megascrewup."

"What are you talking about?"

He mumbled, "Research is the key. Most of the time."

Even though she had had no idea what he meant, she'd said, "Go on. Tell me what went wrong."

"IPO was a bad choice. Who knew?"

"I don't understand. Can you talk more plainly?"

A long silence followed her request. "You might be sorry you asked."

"I won't be."

She recalled uttering those words with complete confidence, unaware that he would soon shock her.

"Nobody stops me from getting what's mine."

"Is that what somebody did?"

"Oh, yeah."

She remembered his fists clenching and had the first inkling that rage was fueling his agitation. "So what will your response be?"

"I like that blouse you're wearing. The color suits you."

"Thanks, but you're trying to change the subject."

He let out a low chuckle. "Is that what I'm doing?"

"Tell me what you intend to do about this problem person of yours."

"Why do you assume I'm going to do anything?"

"Because turning the other cheek isn't your style."

"You think?"

"I think I'm not in the mood for games. If you don't want to be open with me, then it's time for you to leave."

"But I've only been here for ten minutes," he objected.

"I see no point in wasting more of my time. The choice is yours."

He had looked disconcerted by her ultimatum, but she'd grown sick of sessions that went nowhere. Andy Forrester wasn't the only agent who gave her the runaround.

"What's your decision?" she asked. "Are you willing to discuss the situation with me?"

"No reason to. I've already figured out a permanent fix to the problem."

Even now, the memory of his sly smile sent a shiver up her spine.

"What do you mean?"

He had stared at her, his eyes as devoid of humanity as those of a snake.

Suddenly, she had known Andy Forrester posed an imminent threat to an unknown party.

"Who's on the receiving end of your 'permanent fix'?" she demanded.

"You don't need to worry about that."

"Tell me who it is."

The tape reproduced his theatrical sigh. "I'm

just making an observation, doc. No need to get all worked up."

"I think we need to consider why you're so angry and find a way to—"

A piercing wail had made further conversation impossible. The fire alarm.

Later, she'd learned there was no fire, that some prankster had pulled the alarm. But by then the damage had been done. Forrester had refused to continue the session. However, his "permanent fix" remark coupled with his cold eyes and sly smile had her believing him capable of violence, possibly murder. So she'd arranged for him to be taken to Ridsdale for a full assessment.

She rewound the tape and played it again, this time cranking up the volume and stopping at intervals throughout their conversation. Forrester's references to "MIOG op" and "IPO" remained unfathomable, but her anxiety deepened. A would-be killer wouldn't take kindly to her interference.

Had Forrester been the shooter last night? Gene believed the man wanted to harm her, and Brent clearly thought Forrester was responsible for the bullets that had smashed through her window, but she still wasn't convinced.

During their first session, Forrester had openly admitted that after growing up in foster care, he had joined the FBI because he wanted respect. Then he'd asked her what she thought was fair compensation for risking his life. She hadn't known how to answer him, but the question had prompted her to delve deeper into his priorities since it was apparent the financial aspect of the job had not lived up to his expectations.

Money was a recurring issue with him. One bitter childhood memory was of his third foster mother stealing his paper route money. He had contemplated pouring drain opener in her drink, but fear of her boyfriend's rock-hard fists had stopped him from doing it. Forrester might kill if he felt cheated out of money, but not because she'd sent him to Ridsdale for a few days. The outburst to the nurse had been angry venting, not proof of deadly intent toward her.

Of course, her opinion would have to change if physical evidence linked him to the crime scene that encompassed her house.

A tantalizing smell redirected her thoughts to her immediate surroundings. Was that coffee? Brent must be awake. She could use a cup. Or three. But to get to the coffee, she'd have to see Brent, and she wasn't sure she wanted to do that just yet. Following his revelations the night before, he'd clammed up, then stalked off to his room.

She'd made her way to the other bedroom, the one that had been Sanderson's. Even though she was exhausted, she'd had trouble falling asleep, her mind filled with unanswered questions and images, many of them involving her cabinmate.

The unwelcome attraction she felt continued to baffle her. And her late-night sensual fantasies starring Brent had to be a manifestation of stress. She certainly wasn't going to have hot, grinding sex with him to relieve it. If the symptoms persisted, she would try a different solution. Like a career change.

She checked her watch. 9:04 a.m. She'd been awake and without caffeine for over an hour. Time for a break. Maybe even time to admit she needed assistance deciphering Forrester's tapes.

The obvious person to do that was Brent Young. He and Forrester worked in the same office, shared the same FBI training and job classification. If Forrester was using work-related jargon—which she suspected was the case—Brent would be familiar with it. That might lead to the person Forrester blamed for wronging him.

Last night, she'd been too rattled to ask Brent what he knew about Forrester. And even if she had, he hadn't been in a communicative frame of mind after their conversation about Sanderson.

Hopefully, this morning they could start off fresh.

Because if he couldn't help her decode Forrester's cryptic words, someone would die.

"GOOD MORNING."

Brent finished pouring coffee into a mug before turning from the counter.

Claire stood in the doorway, her dark blond

hair falling in soft waves to her shoulders. Her green eyes looked clear and alert as if she'd been up for a while, and he wondered why it had taken her so long to emerge from the other bedroom. Was the prospect of his company so distasteful?

The thought bothered him more than it should have, which irked him further.

"That smells good," she said, gesturing to the coffee.

"Help yourself." He stalked over to the oak table on the far side of the kitchen. His job was to protect her, not fetch and carry for her. He might as well make that clear.

If she noticed his brusque tone, she gave no sign of it as she wandered over to the cupboards and checked through them.

"There's sugar next to the stove," he said, relenting. "But if you want cream, you'll have to wait until we pick up groceries later."

"That's okay. I take mine black."

After she'd filled a mug with coffee, she turned and leaned against the counter. "How well do you know Andy Forrester?"

After their disagreement over Forrester's involvement in last night's events, her question surprised him. "We've attended the same staff meetings, but I've never worked an assignment with him, if that's what you're asking."

"Have you ever talked to him outside of work? Maybe gone out for a beer with him?"

"Nope, can't say that I have." He tipped his chair back against the wall. "In retrospect, I'm glad. If I'm going to be shot at, I'd rather it's done by a stranger than a friend."

Claire frowned, apparently disappointed with his answer.

"You think that's a bad attitude?"

She shook her head. "I didn't say that." Her

tone implied that he was getting his back up over nothing.

Maybe so, but it was hard for him not to feel defensive in the presence of a psychologist. "You're the one he shared his deep, dark secrets with."

She stared at her coffee. "He said only enough to alarm me. But he didn't stay at Ridsdale long enough for a full psychological evaluation—"

"Psychological evaluations are a load of crap."

She lifted an eyebrow. "And you know this because…?"

He smiled tightly. "We're not here for you to question me."

"Look, I'm sorry if you had a negative experience—"

The "negative experience" she alluded to had almost wrecked his life. But he had no intention of unloading his personal history to an FBI shrink.

"Nobody can know what Forrester is capable of just because of some boxes ticked *yes* on a questionnaire."

"Is that how you think I evaluate patients?" she sputtered.

No doubt about it. This time, she was the one feeling defensive. That was a whole lot better than her believing they were buddies just because they'd escaped from her house together.

A muscle twitched in Claire's jaw, but when she spoke her voice was calm. "I don't use questionnaires. I ask whatever questions I think will give me an understanding of the patient."

Nice recovery. He caught himself wondering if she ever lost control—and not just of her temper. Because something about her suggested she kept a lot more than anger bottled up inside her.

What would it take for her to let loose? He wanted to witness that explosion. Hell, he wanted to trigger it.

"I even tape our conversations," she said, "so I can listen to them again later."

"Is that legal?" he asked, goading her just because he felt like it.

"With my patient's consent." Her tone was still mild, but she set her mug on the counter with a solid thunk. "Wow, you really don't like psychologists, do you?"

He folded his arms across his chest. "I'd have to tick the yes box on that one."

She considered him for a long moment. Then her lips curved in a smile. "Well, at least you're honest about it. Which is more than I can say for some people."

Her words defused a little bit of his resentment, and he found himself wanting to smile back at her. He frowned instead.

She shifted uneasily. "If this assignment is a problem for you, maybe Gene could find somebody else—"

"How I feel about your profession won't affect my ability to protect you. As I proved last night."

"You saved my life," she agreed. "Now I'm hoping you can do the same for Forrester's other target."

"How am I supposed to do that? You said you don't know who it is."

"The case I brought with me last night contains tapes of my sessions with Forrester."

Brent gave a low whistle. "No wonder he came to your house. He wanted to get rid of you *and* your tapes."

She flinched.

For a moment, he was sorry he'd been so

blunt. He pushed the regret aside. He always called a spade a spade. Claire should get used to that about him. "I want to listen to them."

She smiled faintly.

He racked his brain but couldn't come up with anything amusing about her situation. "What am I missing?"

She shrugged. "After the way you dismissed psychologists and their methods, I wasn't sure you'd be willing to help me."

"Just what kind of help are you talking about?"

"I don't understand certain terms Forrester used," she admitted. "I'm hoping you will."

Even though he knew it was a cheap shot, he couldn't resist. "And I thought shrinks had all the answers."

She turned and walked down the hall. "Not this one."

He caught himself admiring her honesty

and humility—and the way her jeans hugged her backside. Dangerous thinking. Especially since the two of them were stuck alone together in a remote cabin. A few minutes later, she returned to the kitchen table with the tapes and player. While she fiddled with the equipment, he tried not to notice the long curve of her neck or the shadowed cleavage revealed by her tank top—and failed miserably. She wasn't trying to entice him. But the effect was every bit as powerful. He cursed under his breath as his trousers became uncomfortably tight.

She handed him the headphones, but he needed a moment to refocus before listening to the tape. "Why would Forrester admit to anything incriminating?"

"I think his ego got in the way, and he let slip more than he intended to."

"Or maybe he was yanking your chain."

"That was my first reaction, too, but I changed my mind. Listen for yourself."

When he had the headphones in place, she started the tape.

After he'd listened to it twice, she asked, "What do you think?"

"The tape's ambiguous, but after last night, I agree that he's dangerous."

"Can you explain 'MIOG op' to me?"

He scratched the back of his neck. "MIOG refers to the FBI Manual of Investigative Operations and Guidelines. So a perfect MIOG op would be an operation that goes like clockwork."

"Any idea which operation he's referring to?"

"Maybe it's one he worked on recently. I'll ask Gene to review Forrester's timesheets."

"Could he have been involved in a financial

investigation?" she asked. "That might explain his reference to an IPO."

He shook his head. "The Cincinnati office doesn't handle them."

"If IPO isn't an initial public offering, then what is it?"

"I don't know," he admitted. "It isn't any FBI acronym that I've heard of."

She pressed her fingers against her lips, clearly distraught. "Why did he have to talk in riddles? I can't stop him from killing if I don't know who's at risk."

He felt as if he were letting her down by not being able to figure out more of Forrester's comments. Except he didn't owe her anything, apart from keeping her safe.

But Claire's wasn't the only life at risk.

He headed for the hall to call Gene, but at the doorway, he happened to glance back. Claire's green eyes were fixated on his body, her lips parted as if breathing were an effort.

He stopped, paralyzed by her hungry stare. A blast of warmth licked along his shoulders and spread through his chest. The burn turned south, traveling into his belly, then lower...

She blinked and looked down at the table. As she gathered up the headset, recorder and tape, he checked her hands. Rock-solid steady. No telltale tremors of arousal. He'd been wrong. She hadn't been throwing out all that heat. He turned back toward the hall, irritated that he'd misread her so completely. But he'd only moved a few strides when he heard something clatter to the floor.

Hah. Her hands weren't so steady, after all.

No longer irritated, he called Gene. Having already informed his supervisor of the shooting at Claire's house last night and their safe arrival at the cabin, his words were brief and direct. "I want to search Forrester's place."

As usual, Gene was all over the situation. "I had the warrant drawn up right after he escaped from Ridsdale. There's a surveillance team watching his house, in case he shows up. I'll let them know to expect you and Claire."

Hold on. His plans hadn't included Claire tagging along. "I think I should go alone."

"And leave Claire on her own?"

"She's safe here."

"What if Forrester saw you last night?"

"No amount of digging will connect me to the cabin. It's still registered to that offshore holding company Sanderson set up." His mentor had been fanatical about privacy after a suspect had killed a colleague in her home.

"Claire should remain with you."

"Gene—"

"That point's not negotiable. The only reason

I'm letting you go is because the department's short three agents. If you want to check out his house, you take her with you."

When Gene pulled rank, no amount of arguing could change his mind. "What's the address?"

Gene gave it to him. Also, a description of the surveillance team's vehicle and both agents' cell numbers. He added, "I'll update them. What's your ETA?"

"Tell them to expect us around noon," Brent said, and disconnected.

Damn. He'd planned on giving Claire a wide berth today. Instead, the trip to Forrester's meant they'd be together for most of the afternoon.

Plenty of time for her to try poking around his brain.

Plenty of time for him to try figuring out if the attraction he felt for her was mutual.

Who would end up with the most interesting revelations?

Claire might have the psych degree, but he'd interrogated lots of tough suspects over the years. If nothing else, it should make for an interesting trip.

He smiled for the first time that morning.

How much did Dr. Lamont really know? Enough to jeopardize his plan?

The psychologist excelled at drawing out thoughts and feelings. No easy feat considering the tough-minded agents who were her patients. And it wasn't as if many of them sought her out on their own. Supervisors usually had to order their staff to meet with her. At least the first time.

Then a lot of the guys figured out there were worse ways to pass the time than hanging out with the lovely Claire Lamont. So they signed up to see her again and again, assuming they could stonewall her.

But she didn't tolerate idle talk for long. She wanted to know it all—the good, the bad and the ugly. Who'd have guessed a few conversations would cause so much trouble?

He should have put an end to it sooner.

That miscalculation had placed the whole operation at risk.

Next time he set out to kill her, he'd do it right.

Chapter Three

Jim Sharratt had lied to the FBI.

The joints in his hands throbbed as he watched his six-year-old granddaughter, Amy, play on the swings at Cambridge Park. He could call them and come clean, but he knew he wouldn't. If his family and friends found out what he'd done, they'd lose respect for him. His son might never allow him to take Amy for another outing.

"See me go really high, Grandpa," she shouted, her skinny, pale legs stretching forward. "I'm flying."

"You sure are, angel." He smiled at her even though he felt like crying. These moments were what he lived for. He couldn't bear to have them taken away from him.

Telling the truth would destroy his life. All because he'd made one terrible error in judgment. Thank God his wife, Jeannie, would never know the man she'd married was capable of such wickedness. He missed her so much. For decades he'd worked eighteen-hour days, six days a week. Jeannie hadn't complained through the lean years, but later on she'd grown unhappy with rarely seeing him. She hadn't wanted more houses or cars or money. She'd wanted more time with him. He'd told her to hang on, just a few more deals...

His retirement had come too late for them to enjoy it. A month before he'd sold off his businesses, Jeannie had caught a virus that became pneumonia and took her life. They couldn't travel the world or laze on the beach or visit with friends as he'd promised her. And all the wealth he'd accumulated over the years couldn't ease his crushing grief and loneliness.

If only Jeannie hadn't died, he would have stayed strong, not become weak and vulnerable to temptation.

Amy giggled, the sound jerking him out of the past.

She swung in a wide arc, her face tilted toward the sun, her fine hair streaming down her back like liquid gold. "Are you thinking what I'm thinking?" she called out to him.

"What's that?"

"Ice cream!"

"Butterscotch ripple, two scoops?"

She beamed at him. "You got it, Grandpa."

He watched her slow the momentum of the swing. Her sneakers skidded to a stop in the loose dirt, then she was racing toward him. A moment later, he swept her up in his arms and breathed in the scent of sunshine and innocence.

Did he have to lose everything because he'd messed up once? No, he refused to believe that. He would carry on as though nothing had happened. As long as he remained silent, that might be possible.

CLAIRE STARED out the passenger window at the trees whipping past. She'd been surprised to learn they were returning to Cincinnati to search Forrester's house. She had just assumed they would wait at the cabin until he was arrested. Apparently Brent wasn't content to do that. In addition to protecting her, he was determined to uncover Forrester's other target.

She glanced sideways at her companion. His straight, black hair was cut short in a no-

nonsense style that matched the expression in his brown eyes. Even though she knew better, his digs about her profession had stung. What had happened to make him feel so negative toward psychology? Had a suspect he'd arrested gotten off because of a psychologist's testimony? Had a friend's mental illness been misdiagnosed?

If she knew the basis for Brent's hostility, she might be able to help him reevaluate the experience. Of course, getting him to open up wasn't going to be easy. But then, few agents arrived at her office ready to pour out their hearts and souls. She had to build trust slowly.

"Most of the agents I know dreamed of a career with the Bureau when they were young," she said. "Was that the case for you, too?"

"Pretty much," he admitted.

"How long have you been an agent?"

"Seven years."

She judged him to be in his late thirties, so his answer surprised her. "Why did you wait so long to apply?"

He frowned. "Who says I waited?"

"Well, I'm guessing you were older than the average recruit when you joined. There must be a reason for that."

"Oh, there's a reason, all right," he muttered.

She waited for an answer that didn't come. Finally, she prompted, "Are you going to give me a hint?"

Silence from the other side of the car.

She'd wanted to get him talking but had struck a nerve instead. Nice going, Freud.

"Let me ask you a question," he said. "When you were a kid, did you dream of becoming a shrink?"

She wasn't fond of the word *shrink,* but maybe if she volunteered some information, he'd reciprocate. "Actually, I dreamed of becoming a veterinarian."

"What made you change your mind?" he asked.

Her brain responded immediately, but she pressed her lips together so her secret couldn't slip out.

"Claire?"

She drew in a deep breath and held it, waiting for the sharp pang to recede to the more familiar ache she'd learned to live with. Oh, God. The loss shouldn't hurt so much. Not after all these years. But it still did.

She made a fist in her lap, released her breath slowly. "I lost interest."

"Why psychology?" he prompted, braking for a slow-moving vehicle.

Leave it alone. But she knew he wouldn't. "I wanted to help people cope with the challenges in their lives."

How idealistic she'd been at twenty. How dis-couraged she felt at this point in her career.

"Do you think you have?" Brent asked.

She'd been struggling with that question for almost a year. *Was* she having a positive impact on her patients? If she accepted that job in Minneapolis, she wouldn't have to agonize anymore. In the meantime, she wasn't about to broadcast her doubts to someone who was already pre-disposed to think badly of her profession. "I think I've been successful with many of my patients."

"Like Forrester?"

Her temper rose. She ignored it, reminding herself that Brent was only doing what she often did: ask probing questions. "By com-mitting Forrester to Ridsdale, I gave him the opportunity to be thoroughly assessed. I also ensured his safety as well as that of his intended target. Now that he's out, who knows what might happen."

"You're not responsible for Forrester's actions," Brent said quietly.

Leaning her head back against the headrest, she closed her eyes. "I'm sorry about earlier. I wasn't trying to pry."

"What were you trying to do?"

She didn't want to admit her real motive so she said, "Make conversation."

"Are you sure that's all?"

She opened her eyes. "What do you mean?"

"You ask a lot of personal questions."

"I'm curious about you."

He changed lanes to pass a blue minivan. "I think it's more than curiosity."

"Like what?"

His soft chuckle made her mouth go dry. "Like maybe you're hot for me."

Her jaw dropped, and heat crept up her neck. "You are so wrong."

"Then explain why your pulse races when I touch you."

"If you're referring to last night at my house, don't forget I thought you were Forrester."

"Only for a couple of seconds. Then you knew it was me, and your heart beat even faster."

Damn, he had noticed. The fact that he spoke the truth only made her more determined to deny it. "You misinterpreted what you felt."

"Is that so?" His hand left the steering wheel and settled on her forearm.

His fingers slid down toward her wrist in a gentle caress. Even though she knew his move was calculated, she couldn't control her accelerating heart rate. Why was she reacting so intensely? He was hardly touching her.

She willed herself to ignore him and focus on the scenery rushing past the car.

A moment later, he turned his head and spoke in a husky voice. "How about we pull over…"

And do what? Her heart went wild at the possibilities.

"…and check out that pulse of yours?"

Shrugging off his hand, she said more sharply than she intended, "Watch the road. I saw a deer-crossing sign a few yards back."

She stared straight ahead, hoping he'd take the hint.

"Sooner or later you're going to run out of excuses to avoid the attraction between us."

His self-satisfied tone irked her. "Are you familiar with the term 'delusional'?"

"Are you familiar with the term 'coward'?"

Her head whipped around. "What?"

"Why can't you be honest about your feelings instead of hiding behind that psychobabble?"

"Psychobabble?" she said. "Why on earth would I be attracted to somebody who disparages what I do for a living?"

He had the gall to smile. "I don't know."

The man was impossible. No matter how much she denied the sparks between them, he wouldn't believe her. But maybe she could convince him that the point was moot. "Even if I were attracted to you, nothing would happen between us."

"Why not?"

"Given my position, it would be wrong to become personally involved—"

"—with a patient. I'm not a patient."

"Not now."

"Not ever," he amended tartly.

"Doesn't matter. I consider all agents to be off limits."

He gave her a penetrating stare. "Why?"

"I have a rule about it."

"Haven't you heard? Rules are made—"

"—to be broken." She shook her head. "Hardly reassuring words coming from a federal agent." But she couldn't prevent the hint of a smile that curved her lips. "You're supposed to enforce the law."

"Hey, I follow the rules in my job."

"Like breaking and entering my house?"

He grinned. "Sometimes the rules require liberal interpretation."

"Does Gene know that?"

"Gene knows I'd never cut the wrong corner."

"Glad to hear it."

"My personal life is a different story," he told her. "There, I don't worry about rules. I go with my impulses."

And what impulses would those be? she couldn't help but wonder. It would be better not to speculate. She was already finding him dangerously appealing. "I commend your flexible approach. But it doesn't change how I feel."

"Maybe you're harboring resentment against *my* profession. And that's the real reason you don't date FBI guys."

"You're entitled to your opinion," she said with a shrug. "However wrong it may be."

A sign appeared on the side of the road, indicating they'd arrived at the outskirts of the city.

The last few minutes had distracted her, but now a shiver ran up her spine. Until Forrester was in custody, she wouldn't feel safe here. But her fear didn't matter. What mattered was tracking down his target before he did.

She only hoped they weren't already too late.

BRENT DRUMMED HIS THUMBS on the steering wheel. Claire's conviction not to get involved with an agent intrigued him. What was she hiding? Because he was certain she was hiding more than her feelings for him. Had she been burned before, maybe in a relationship with one of his colleagues? The possibility made him uncomfortable. He didn't go for long-term relationships, but a woman who became involved with him did so knowing the score. Lots of men made promises they had no intention of keeping. Is that what had happened to make Claire wary?

Or maybe her "rule" was just a smoke-screen? A way of not having to admit she was attracted to him. What did psychologists call that? Denial?

He, on the other hand, had no problem owning up to the attraction he felt. Their disagreements revved his engine because she was smart and focused. Her mouth looked infinitely kissable, and her thick, blond hair was sure to feel amazing against his bare skin. Last, but certainly not least, her curves had him hungering to learn every contour.

She didn't know him well enough to realize that telling him about her "rule" had been a tactical error. He never accepted rules at face value. They always had to make sense to him. This one didn't. This one seemed more like a challenge. And he never backed down from one of those.

Thinking of challenges reminded him of Forrester's comments on the tape. What had happened to bend the bastard so out of shape? And whose life was in danger? Of course, the most pertinent question right now was, would a search of his house be productive or a colossal waste of time?

As he turned the corner onto Forrester's street, he counted a dozen vehicles parked along the curb, including the one assigned to the surveillance team. He pulled into an empty spot and called the number Gene had given him.

"Riley Harris," a voice answered.

The name wasn't familiar, but frequent transfers made it hard to keep track of everyone in the Cincinnati office. Brent identified himself.

"Gene said you'd be checking in," the other man said.

"Any sign of Forrester?"

"Negative. McKenna's walking the perimeter. If Forrester shows up, he'll attempt to talk him into giving himself up."

It was worth a try, Brent supposed. And Alec McKenna had been around long enough to know not to let down his guard.

"I'll let McKenna know you've arrived," Harris said.

Brent closed his cell phone and turned to Claire. She hadn't spoken since they'd reached the city and was hugging her arms to her body even though it wasn't cold in the car.

"Don't worry," he said. "The surveillance team hasn't seen any sign of Forrester."

She nodded, but her arms remained locked across her torso.

He cupped her shoulder with his palm, drew her gaze to meet his. "If he shows his face, you have me and two other agents to protect you. But it's more likely he's gone to ground miles from here." He didn't know if that was true—all he knew was that he felt compelled to ease Claire's tension.

"I hope you're right," she said. "Leaving town may force him to postpone going after the person on the tape."

He checked his gun just in case he was wrong. "Let's go."

They didn't encounter Alec McKenna on their way to the back of the house, but Brent hadn't expected to. The agent would be focused on watching out for Forrester, and their presence couldn't act as a distraction.

At the house, Brent picked the lock on the front door, then he and Claire ventured inside. The main level consisted of a galley-style kitchen and an L-shaped living-room-and-dining-room area. A quick search through the stacks of opened mail on the coffee table revealed utility bills and junk mail, certainly nothing of interest. He checked the garage next. Empty. Wordlessly, he motioned for Claire to proceed to the second floor.

"What a mess," Claire murmured, advancing into the room at the top of the stairs.

The space, which had been set up as a home office, overflowed with books, magazines and loose papers. Suddenly, he was glad Gene had made him bring Claire along. Two people could search through this pigsty faster than one.

The office door slid shut.

Claire crossed the room to reopen it. "Where do you want me to start?"

"Try the stack of paper next to the bookcase," he said, his attention caught by the framed photo of Forrester on the desk. Sporting a wide smile, the agent stood next to a shiny classic Trans Am.

The door closed again due to the sloped floor, and this time Claire gave up and left it that way.

Opening the top drawer of the desk, Brent leafed through its contents which included an address book and six months' worth of bank statements. He flipped to the most current one. No immediate red flags. All the deposits and withdrawals appeared to be of reasonable magnitude. Setting the statement aside, he turned to the next one.

Paper rustled in the vicinity of the bookcase. Claire let out a sigh.

"Find anything interesting?" he asked.

"Only if car specifications and parts catalogues float your boat. Forrester mentioned in one of our sessions that classic cars were his hobby, but it looks more like an obsession."

Brent moved on to the bottom drawer where he found a nearly empty briefcase and a stack of credit-card receipts. It would take hours to review all the receipts, and he didn't want to spend that much time here.

He placed the address book, credit-card receipts and bank statements inside the briefcase, then added the photo from the desk.

"It's getting stuffy in here," she murmured, moving past him.

She unlocked the room's solitary window, then tugged on the handles without success.

"The house is old. It's probably been painted shut," he commented.

She headed for the closed door as he added more items to the briefcase.

A sudden cry jolted him like an electrical charge.

"The knob's hot," Claire said, regarding her upturned palm in disbelief.

In a heartbeat, he stood beside her, pressing his ear against the door. From the other side came a crackling sound. His gaze shot to the woman who should have been safe at the cabin, but was trapped here with him instead.

He answered the unspoken question in her eyes with a single word.

"Fire."

Chapter Four

Claire stared at Brent in stunned disbelief. The stinging in her hand receded under a wave of fear as he pulled out his cell phone. He pressed only three buttons. 9-1-1.

Fire. They had to get out.

Instinctively, she reached for the doorknob again.

"No," he yelled, jerking her back against him. "The fire's right outside. If you open the door, it'll explode into the office."

Oh, God. He was right. Hungry for oxygen,

the fire would gravitate toward any new source. They had to find another exit. The window.

"Help me," she said, heading for it.

This time he didn't suggest reasons why it wouldn't open. Turning on his heel, he made it there ahead of her. She watched anxiously as he yanked and pulled.

"It won't…budge," he said, his words interrupted by coughs.

Her own throat felt raw and scratchy. Smoke seeped under the door like fog in a horror movie. She tugged at Brent's arm in alarm.

He glanced over his shoulder, then cursed softly and stripped off his shirt.

The sight of his rippling muscles and bronzed flesh had her mouth going dry—or maybe she was just reacting to the heat building inside the room. She couldn't tear her gaze away as he dropped his shirt to the floor and used his foot to wedge it against the crack. It wasn't going to stop all the smoke, but it might keep out enough so they could breathe for an extra minute or two.

Unless the door went up in flames.

A mighty crack sounded in another part of the house. Could it be the support beams collapsing? She had no way of knowing, and no intention of staying inside long enough to find out. She looked around for a heavy object to break the window, but Brent was already wheeling the oak desk-chair toward her. Lifting it by the arms, he thrust the chunky legs at the window pane repeatedly.

A spray of glass shards rewarded his efforts. Cooler air from outside rushed into the oven the office had become. Claire almost wept with relief as she moved forward, eagerly breathing in the fresh air.

Brent dropped the chair and blocked her path. "Stay away from the opening."

"Why?" All she wanted was some air to ease the burning in her lungs and the stinging in her eyes.

"Because the house didn't burst into flames on its own. The arsonist could be trying to smoke us out."

She instinctively took a step back, away from the window.

"The surveillance team—"

"He must have got past them to torch the house. I don't want to take the chance he picks us off as we leave."

Oh, God. If Brent was right, their only escape route exposed them to another kind of danger.

A gray haze of smoke soon filled the office.

Dragging the neckline of her tank top up to cover her mouth, she sucked air raggedly through the fabric. Her throat was already so raw that every breath she took hurt more than the last. She swayed to one side, dizzy from lack of oxygen. Losing consciousness wasn't far off. And even though her stomach churned at the possibility of being shot, she decided a bullet wound couldn't feel worse than this slow suffocation.

She eyed the narrow opening, psyching up to plunge through it, no matter what she'd encounter on the other side.

Brent must have sensed her intent because he moved to trap her against the wall.

"Trust me," he murmured. "I'll get you out of this alive."

She wouldn't have believed those words from anyone else, but last night this man had proved he could protect her. So even though her instincts screamed for her to shove him out of the way, she didn't surrender to them.

She closed her eyes, breathed shallowly.

Despite the dire situation, she was supremely

conscious of his naked chest. The smooth skin...taut muscles...tangy masculine smell. As his body pressed against hers, his labored breathing mirrored her own.

"Hold on," Brent said. "We'll leave when the emergency crews arrive. Whoever set this fire won't risk being spotted."

She nodded to show she understood and struggled to stay alert, knowing that her survival depended on reacting quickly to changing circumstances.

Hold on. Hold on.

The words were a mantra in her mind. She clung to them for comfort. Belatedly, she realized that she was also clinging to Brent, her arms locked around his waist. She knew she should release him. She also knew she should be mortified. She had no business touching him, especially after denying her attraction to him in the car. But this wasn't about attraction. This was about need. She needed to be close to him right now. She needed to share his strength, absorb his courage. His lack of fear was the only thing keeping her from full-scale panic.

He didn't seem to mind or even be aware of her fierce embrace. His gaze was directed outside, scanning the area around the house.

Sirens wailed nearby.

"Let's go," he said abruptly.

Claire felt her legs go weak. Finally.

But her relief evaporated when the tongues of flame began to lick at the frame of the door. The spark and crackle of the fire was so close. It wouldn't be long before it had consumed everything in its path.

Brent stepped in front of the window, then paused for a long moment before he grasped her by the waist and hoisted her through the opening in a single, smooth movement. Only when she was kneeling outside on the roof of the garage did she realize why he had stopped in front of the window first—to offer himself as a target. The reminder that Brent would take a bullet for her made her grateful that he was protecting her, and worried what could happen to him.

She waited, expecting him to join her immediately. When he didn't, fear stabbed her. Had he been cut off by the fire? Or had he passed out from smoke inhalation? The thought of climbing back into the burning office terrified her, but she couldn't leave him to die. She gripped the window frame, anxious that she might not be strong enough to drag him to safety.

He appeared in the opening, brandishing Forrester's briefcase like a trophy.

Her happiness at seeing him turned to anger.

"You risked your life for a briefcase? Are you crazy?"

He swung a leg out the window. "I didn't think shrinks liked that word. Too derogatory."

Flames leapt behind him as the fire advanced into the office. So close. Too damn close. The man was in denial about his own mortality.

"I know a lot more derogatory words than 'crazy'," she said, through gritted teeth.

"I'll bet," he said, with a grin. "You can enlighten me later."

He pointed to the street where half a dozen men in protective clothing swarmed around a fire engine. "Those hoses look set to go. Unless you want an impromptu shower, I suggest we get off this roof right away."

Following his lead, she crawled over the shingles to the far side of the roof. But when she saw him swing over the edge, hang by his fingers for a moment, then drop to the ground, she groaned inwardly. There was no way she could do that. Her burned hand hurt so much, she'd probably faint from the pain.

"Throw me the briefcase," he called out.

She did, using her left hand.

Brent looked up at her, waiting. "I know it seems like a long way down, but it's not that far. Jump and I'll catch you."

He obviously thought she was afraid of heights, and she didn't bother to contradict him. Her injury was nothing compared to the ones he'd likely collected over the course of his career.

Rolling onto her stomach, she pushed off the roof. As promised, he caught her before her feet hit the grass.

"Thanks," she said breathlessly. Was it her imagination or did his hands linger on her?

"No problem," he said, releasing her.

Seconds later, a fire hose spewed jets of water onto the east side of the house.

They sprinted across the lawn, then headed for the fire engine, where Brent let the crew know that the house was empty and the fire had likely been started by its owner, who was wanted by the FBI.

Reminded of the surveillance team, Claire murmured, "Where do you suppose your colleagues are?"

"I don't know," Brent said grimly, "but I intend to find out."

He strode along the street past numerous parked cars until he reached a green Chevy Impala. Peering through the window, he let out a guttural curse.

"What is it?" Claire said, unable to see past him into the car.

"Harris has been shot." He opened the door and reached inside.

She glimpsed bloody clothing and a slumped-over body before she turned away, sickened. "How bad is it?"

"He's dead."

Oh, God. She swallowed. "Where's McKenna?"

"Let's go find out."

For the next ten minutes, they trekked through the surrounding yards, climbed over fences and checked behind hedges. Nobody objected to their presence, perhaps because those who might have were distracted by the fire engine in front of Forrester's house. With every step, Claire felt a deepening sense of dread. A few minutes later, they rounded the corner of a garage and found a man lying face down on the grass. Blood oozed from his scalp, matting his dark red hair.

She held her breath as Brent knelt beside him and touched the side of his neck.

"I feel a pulse," he said.

McKenna's eyelashes flickered and the lips under a generous mustache uttered a groan. "What the hell?" he muttered.

"I was hoping you'd tell me," Brent said.

"All I know is my head feels ready to explode."

"You're lucky to be alive. Harris isn't."

"Sonovabitch." The agent sat up gingerly. "Did you see who did this?"

Brent shook his head. "I just came from the house." He explained about the fire and how he and Claire had escaped onto the roof of the garage.

McKenna exhaled heavily. "How the hell did he get past me?"

"Forrester knows all the tricks."

"I can't believe he'd do this. I've worked with him a few times, and I liked him."

"That probably explains why you're still

alive," Brent said. "He knew you, but Harris was a stranger to him."

"Being locked up must have messed with his mind," McKenna muttered.

"You believe he'd kill a fellow agent because of two days at Ridsdale?" Claire asked incredulously.

McKenna treated her to a long, hard stare. Did he resent her for confining Forrester to a psychiatric facility? After the roller-coaster events of the last hour, she was uncertain how to interpret his expression.

McKenna fingered his bloody scalp.

"You should see the paramedics," she said.

"Nah. A couple of Tylenol, and I'll be fine."

She wasn't surprised he'd refuse medical treatment. He was, after all, a G-man. Too stubborn and proud to admit to any human frailties. Just like her father had been before his breakdown.

The memory of her father had her clenching her fists. But the pain it dredged up was superceded by a more immediate one: the blistered skin on her right palm. She relaxed her hands immediately and bit her lip to keep from voicing her discomfort.

"You'd better head to the hospital," Brent said to the injured agent. "Gene won't let you get back to work without a doctor's okay."

"Waste of time, in my opinion, but you're right."

"While you're doing that, I'm going after Forrester."

"If you find him, don't underestimate him."

"I'm not the one with the concussion," Brent said.

McKenna grimaced. "Good point."

As Claire walked with Brent back to his car, she asked, "Why would Forrester set fire to his own home?"

Brent laid the briefcase in his trunk and rummaged through his gym bag for a T-shirt. "There must have been something inside he wanted destroyed."

She watched the muscles in his bare back shift with his movements, remembering the feel of his supple skin, the tangy scent of his sweat. As he raised his arms to tug on his shirt, her mind stalled out, and she had to shake herself mentally to restart it. "You mean us?"

"Or incriminating evidence."

"I think he's too smart for that."

"He didn't expect you to commit him to Ridsdale."

"He's an experienced agent. He knows to be prepared for the unexpected."

"You have a better theory?"

A full minute ticked by as she tried to come up with a plausible one.

"Not at this point," she admitted. "But I don't believe Forrester set fire to his home or killed Harris. The agent I interviewed wouldn't risk prison without a huge financial incentive."

Brent shrugged, then strode toward the neighboring house. She hurried to catch up.

A middle-aged couple stood in the driveway, watching the comings and goings of the firefighters with keen interest.

Brent introduced Claire and then himself.

The woman's pale blue eyes widened. "What's the FBI doing at a house fire?"

Brent sidestepped her question. "I didn't catch your name, ma'am."

"Jolene Blackburne. And this is my husband, Rod." She patted the sleeve of the man's yellow T-shirt with obvious affection.

Brent jotted down the information. "Are you

well acquainted with the person who lives next door?"

"Andy Forrester keeps his grass cut and his trash inside till garbage day. Got no complaints with him. Unlike some others around here." Lips twisted in disgust, she glared at the house directly across the street.

"When did you last see him?"

Jolene turned to her husband. "A couple of days ago, right, hon?"

Her husband nodded.

She heaved a sigh, her gaze resting on the still-burning hulk that was Forrester's residence. "A terrible thing for him to come home to. Do you know how it started?"

Claire figured Brent would plead ignorance, so his next words surprised her.

"Looks like it might be arson."

"Arson? Oh, my God. Did you hear that, Rod?"

The man rolled his eyes. "I'm standing right here, Jolene. Of course I heard."

The woman pressed her fingers to her lips. "That could have been our house up in flames. All our furniture, photographs, my mother's Royal Doulton china, every last thing burned to a crisp." Her distraught expression changed to angry speculation. "Was it kids playing with matches?"

"I don't think so," Brent said. "Did you see anybody around his house today?"

Rod scratched under his baseball cap. "Nope. But I worked the late shift last night so I was sleeping until the sirens woke me up."

"And I was doing laundry in the basement all morning." She added, "What about his fancy car? Did it go up in flames, too?"

"You know he doesn't keep that one in his garage," Rod reminded his wife. "He only brings it home on Sundays to shine her up and show her off."

"What kind of car is it?" Claire asked.

Rod grinned. "A sixty-nine Trans Am."

"That man sure does love his car," Jolene added.

"His prize possession, huh?"

Brent made a quick notation on a business card and gave it to the man. "Thanks for your cooperation. Please call if you see Mr. Forrester or if you remember anything else that might help our investigation."

He headed down the driveway to the street.

Claire waited until they were out of earshot of Forrester's neighbors. "Too bad they didn't see who set the fire."

He stared straight ahead, but she wasn't sure whether he was deep in thought or ignoring her.

"Brent? Are you okay?"

His pace quickened. "I'm not comfortable with this setup. You're supposed to be under protection, not out in the field interviewing contacts."

"I barely took part in the conversation." She lengthened her strides to match his. "The car is worth following up on, don't you think?"

"Maybe," Brent admitted.

When she started to speak again, he cut her off. "Look, I appreciate your wanting to help, but this isn't your concern."

Her temper flared at his tone, and she stopped walking abruptly. "Anything that could help the FBI locate Forrester *is* my concern."

"Let me rephrase that. You did your job. You determined that Forrester was a threat and sent him to Ridsdale. Now you have to trust Gene and me to do our job, which is to ascertain his whereabouts and apprehend him."

"I thought your job was to protect me."

He locked gazes with her, and she suddenly felt light-headed. A delayed reaction to nearly suffocating earlier, she decided. It was *not* because his dark, thick-lashed eyes took her breath away.

"You are my primary responsibility," Brent said, "but I intend to participate in the search for Forrester."

Was that annoyance she heard in his voice? Did he feel that safeguarding her was diverting him from a more important job?

She forced her thoughts back to his last comment. "I'm sure he'll be caught faster if you participate."

He nodded. "I'm glad we agree on something."

She smiled at the first sign of accord between them. It lasted until he spoke again.

"You can forget about my discussing field

operations with you. As I said before, that's not your concern. The only thing you need to know is that the Bureau will do everything possible to bring Forrester into custody."

Easy for him to say. He wasn't expected to wait passively for the situation to be resolved.

Watching others act while she did nothing went against her grain. Especially when it looked to her like Forrester's arrest was far from imminent.

Chapter Five

Brent kept a tight rein on his frustration until he was behind the closed door of Gene's office. "Claire shouldn't have been at Forrester's."

"Her being there wasn't the problem," his boss countered, shoving a handful of papers into his out tray. "The problem was the surveillance team that failed to stop a perp from torching his house."

"They followed Bureau procedures that Forrester, being an insider, is completely familiar with." He wasn't making excuses for his col-

leagues, just pointing out the extenuating circumstances.

Gene glanced up, his pale eyes unyielding,
his salt-and-pepper hair reminding Brent that
the man had thirty years of experience deal-
ing with tough situations. "The team's failure
endangered lives."

There was one life that had been placed in
jeopardy needlessly. "Harris and McKenna
didn't veto Claire remaining at the cabin. That
was you." The decision had almost had fatal
consequences, and he wanted his boss to admit
he'd made a mistake. "Dammit, she could have
died in that fire."

The other man's eyes narrowed and his voice
boomed like a drill sergeant's. "She escaped
without a scratch. You know why? Because I
assigned the right damn agent to watch over
her."

It was a new experience to be yelled at and

complimented at the same time. Before he could shift gears and respond, Gene barked out, "Until I'm convinced she's not in danger, Claire isn't to be left alone anywhere, anytime. No exceptions. If you're not happy with bodyguard duty, I'll assign somebody else."

Another agent taking care of Claire?

His reaction was visceral, involuntary. "Don't even think about replacing me," he ground out, fists clenched at his sides. "She's my responsibility."

Gene stared at him hard. Then he dropped his gaze and carried on with organizing his desk. "Fine. She's yours for the duration."

His satisfaction with Gene's decision was diluted by annoyance that he'd admitted possessive feelings toward the department's psychologist.

"Where's Claire now?" Gene inquired.

"With Lisa."

"Tell me what you found at the house."

Brent opened Forrester's briefcase and withdrew the photo of the agent with his cherished Trans Am. "I thought a candid shot of Forrester would be useful when I canvassed his neighborhood. However, it turns out the vehicle in the picture is very important to him."

"Are our tech guys working on it?"

"The car wasn't at the house. His neighbors don't know where he keeps it."

"I'll have Mickey look for it," Gene said, jotting down a note. "What about Forrester? Any leads on him?"

"I snagged his address book. Only a few names to check out."

"I'll free up some manpower to do that. What else?"

"Forrester's Trans Am is a classic. Extremely expensive. I'm wondering how he had the money to buy it."

"Maybe he borrowed big. Or has a rich lady friend who likes to buy him gifts. He could have a source of income apart from his Bureau wages. Possibly illegal," Gene mused.

"We have his bank account and credit card statements. They might give some insight into his financial situation."

Gene frowned. "I'm not optimistic we're going to find him with our usual methods. He knows how we search for a fugitive—who we contact, what we look for, how we process info."

"He has an unpredictable streak," Brent agreed. "He's already demonstrated that."

As well as a willingness to kill.

If they didn't catch him fast, he would surely up the body count.

THROUGH THE CLOSED DOOR of Gene's office, Claire could hear the sound of loud voices.

Lisa Conrad, Gene's admin assistant, glanced up from her computer monitor. "Don't look so worried. Gene and Brent get riled up from time to time."

Claire nodded, then sipped the coffee she'd bought from the vending machine around the corner.

Leaning across her workstation, Lisa lowered her voice to a conspiratorial whisper. "So what's it like staying alone with Mr. Tough Guy?"

She feigned nonchalance. "Fine."

"That guy's hot," Lisa said, with a grin. "Or haven't you noticed?"

When Claire didn't answer, Lisa winked. "Oh, yeah, you've noticed. Heck, you'd have to be blind not to. The question is, what are you doing about it?"

Claire finished her coffee and tossed the cup in the wastepaper basket. "Agent Young has been assigned to protect me. There's nothing personal between us."

"Then you're wasting a golden opportunity, girl. Most of the women on this floor would be delirious to swap places with you."

Oh no, they wouldn't, Claire thought. Not if they knew she'd almost died twice in the last twenty-four hours. "I didn't realize he was in such high demand."

"Yeah, well, it's not like he even notices. That hunky man shows zero interest in the female staffers around here."

Lisa's words pleased her more than they should have. "Maybe he wants to keep his professional and personal lives separate."

"Could be," Lisa said. "But I bet he'd make an exception for the right woman."

What type of woman would Brent go for? Claire wondered. Certainly not her. She was too intense, too opinionated, too—

She stopped, annoyed that she'd been speculating about him.

"You could be that woman," Lisa continued.

She shook her head. "I don't think so."

"Of course, he'd be a challenge. But your line of work makes you good at connecting with people."

"I haven't had much success with him."

"The other agents like you a lot more than Dr. Telso."

Claire had heard rumors about her predecessor's unpopularity, but she knew for a fact that Brent didn't consider her an improvement. Whenever she touched on subjects of a personal nature, he shut her down or stalked away.

"I appreciate the vote of confidence, but Brent and I are too different to have a relationship."

"Relationships are overrated." Lisa wiggled her eyebrows suggestively. "I was talking about sex."

Claire couldn't help but laugh. "I just met the guy and you think I should fall into bed with him?"

"Fall?" Lisa shook her head. "Hell, honey, I'd jump into bed with him."

"Jump into bed with whom?" Gene asked, bearing down on Lisa's workstation with Brent close behind him.

Claire felt her cheeks flame.

"No one," Lisa said, winking at Claire before she turned her attention back to her monitor and settled her fingers on the keyboard.

Claire felt Brent's gaze on her, but kept her own averted. If she looked at him, he would surely guess they'd been discussing him.

Gene came closer, a concerned expression on his face. "How are you holding up, Claire?"

"Okay," she said, although her hand stung as if she'd stuck it in a beehive. "I'd like to meet with you for a minute, in private."

He turned to Lisa. "While Claire and I are talking, please scan the material Brent gives you so he can load the files onto his laptop."

Gene escorted her into his office and closed the door. "What's up?"

"I heard you and Brent going at it. I couldn't hear what you were saying, but I'm concerned. Was it about me?"

She knew her speculation was on target when Gene hesitated.

"You should know," she went on, "that it's okay with me if Brent wants to be reassigned. He's done a great job, but you shouldn't force him to continue—"

"You've got it all wrong, Claire."

She'd expected the denial, but Gene sounded sincere. "Are you sure?"

"Brent was upset about what went down at Forrester's house. He wants to keep on protecting you. Most definitely."

Relief flooded her. Because no matter how infuriating Brent could be at times, he had saved her life twice and she trusted him to do it again.

"What happened today," Gene said, "was terrible, but you seem to be handling it well."

Mostly because she'd been blocking it out of her mind. And although part of her was still horrified and shaken, another part was keenly aware that the outcome could have been far worse. Even so, Gene had lost one of his men.

"I'm very sorry about Harris," she said.

Gene looked down at his desk. "He was a new agent. Showed a lot of promise."

"You couldn't have prevented what happened."

Gene's solemn gaze lifted to meet hers. "Thanks for your concern, Claire, but I've had men die under my command before. I can deal with it."

"I know you can." She was the one who felt out of her element.

"We'll get Forrester," Gene promised, and the fierceness in his tone left her in no doubt that it would happen.

She cleared her throat. "What about my patients?"

"You're not meeting with anybody until the situation with Forrester is resolved."

"But I have appointments every day."

"Give me your BlackBerry. Lisa will check your schedule and cancel the ones for the rest of this week."

"But—"

"We need to eliminate the risk that Forrester

can trace your calls. Lisa will give you a disposable cell phone on your way out."

"I don't care about phones. I care about my patients."

"Until we rule out the possibility that someone internal is involved with Forrester, I'm not letting you meet with anyone."

She knew Gene was only trying to keep her safe. Still, it was hard to accept not working until Forrester was arrested. What if he eluded them for weeks? Some of her patients were just beginning to trust her. Months of effort could easily slip away. Of course, if she accepted the job offer in Minneapolis, her patients would have to adjust to her absence on a permanent basis.

Gene got to his feet. "Try to make the best of this break, Claire. And know that we're working hard to end it soon."

As BRENT UNLOADED the groceries onto the cabin's kitchen counter, it occurred to him that his companion was uncharacteristically quiet. She stood in front of the fridge, a blank expression on her face.

"Claire?"

He couldn't be certain from this distance, but it seemed as if she was trembling. He should probably say something to settle her down but couldn't think of the right words. Besides, talk was overrated. He was a man of action. But what action was called for?

He eyed her slender frame. If he held her, would the trembling stop?

He remembered the last minutes at Forrester's house when Claire had plastered herself to him like wallpaper. Even now, he could feel her arms around his bare torso, her breasts crushed against his chest, the softness of her skin and the silky texture of her hair. His body began to respond, and he knew he had better avoid physical contact with her.

She blinked several times, on the verge of tears.

Her damp eyes surprised him. She had acted so levelheaded during the fire and the discovery of Harris's body, it was easy to forget how overwhelmed she might be feeling. Wanting to offer some kind of comfort but not trusting himself to embrace her, he reached for her hand.

She cried out, jerking it away from him.

Damn. He'd forgotten all about her touching the hot doorknob—probably because she hadn't drawn attention to it. That type of stoicism was a refreshing change from his last girlfriend, Patty, who had complained about everything: the weather, PMS, his job. Why was he comparing them? He wasn't looking for another girlfriend—no matter how much Claire's hug had turned him on.

"Let me see," he growled, annoyed by his meandering thoughts.

She hesitated for a moment, then extended her right hand to him, palm up.

As he stared at the red, blistered skin, a wave of regret hit him. It was his job to protect her. Not just to keep her alive but to keep her safe. He'd failed her.

That must never happen again.

He guided her over to a kitchen chair, then retrieved the first aid kit from the cupboard above the stove.

"What's that?" Claire asked, peering at the capsules he extracted from the kit.

"Aloe vera." Breaking them open, he spread the gel over the burned area.

He didn't want her to have a scar. When this was all over, he wanted her to forget about

Forrester, not carry a reminder of the violent patient who had tried to kill her.

She bit her lip, obviously hurting, and he spoke to distract her. "I'm surprised there's any of this stuff left. Sanderson used to singe his fingers every time he grilled—" He stopped abruptly.

A very loud silence ticked by.

"It must be difficult to be here without him."

He jerked his shoulder in an awkward shrug. He should know better than to talk to a shrink. She'd immediately zeroed in on his pain.

As he carefully wrapped gauze around her hand, he braced himself for more of her questions.

She surprised him by saying, "You'd make a good paramedic."

His mother was a nurse and had taught him how to bandage cuts, set broken bones. Important skills for a skinny kid who had been beaten by the bullies at school because he sucked at team sports and had no father. "I fought like hell to become an FBI agent. I'm not about to switch careers anytime soon."

"I didn't say you should be a medic. Just that you could be."

Should. Could. Typical shrink double-talk. But instead of ignoring her comment, he heard himself asking, "Why?"

"You stay calm and focused in a crisis." Her voice took on a husky undertone. "And you have a gentle touch."

She dropped her gaze to her bandaged hand, but a telltale pink stained her cheeks.

He smiled as he applied adhesive tape to secure the bandage. So she thought he had a gentle touch, did she? Maybe she'd enjoy it somewhere other than her hand. He traced his fingers from her wrist to her elbow. Her arm was lightly tanned, muting the network of veins under her skin. He thought about tracing those veins with his tongue, then licking places on her body with no tan.

Claire had said she wouldn't get involved with an agent. But she was going to make an exception. For him.

He heard her breath catch as his fingers moved toward her shoulder, and he smiled again. Did she have any idea what he was thinking? What he wanted to do to her? What he wanted her to do to him?

He still distrusted psychologists. But he was making an exception. For her.

Moving closer, he kissed her full on the mouth.

CLAIRE'S MIND SPUN like a kaleidoscope. Feelings she barely recognized swamped her. Feelings of longing. Of need. Of desire. No matter how much she pretended otherwise,

Brent's every look, his every touch sparked an intense awareness in her. The chemistry between them was volatile as nitroglycerine, and she had no doubt his kiss was the prelude to a sweet explosion.

Opening her lips, she welcomed the thrust of his tongue. She'd never been kissed so thoroughly. Her last boyfriend had been a main-event man, with little interest in foreplay. Despite her attempts to guide him otherwise, he'd remained stubbornly fixated on the culmination of the act. That destination-over-journey preference had only been one of the differences that had led to their breakup two years ago.

Brent seemed to be more attuned to her. She rewarded him by kissing him back with enthusiasm, angling her mouth to deepen the kiss and show her approval for his slow, unhurried pace. He let out a low groan. The vibration rippled through every one of her nerve endings.

She wanted to get closer to him. As she moved forward, her breasts brushed against his T-shirt and her nipples puckered. She gasped, thrilled by the sensation.

He kissed her again, then slipped his hand beneath her tank top and stroked the swollen peaks through her bra.

Oh, yeah. That felt good. Better than good. Phenomenal.

But was *phenomenal* enough of a reason to keep going?

This morning Brent had made it clear that he despised psychologists. And during the intervening hours, he'd given no indication of having altered his opinion. So how come she was letting him feel her up? Not only letting him but *encouraging* him? And enjoying herself to boot? The fire at Forrester's place had done more than burn her hand. It had fried her brain.

Brent's fingers traced her spine, en route to the clasp on her bra. Within seconds, he'd have it unfastened and touch her bare breasts. And though her body yearned for exactly that, her brain was struggling to give her a different message. Something about not letting a man she barely knew strip her naked.

She jerked back and dragged her top down.

"What's wrong?"

"What's happening between us," she said.

He shot her a look of disbelief. "You don't want me touching you?"

The lie stuck in her throat, and she swallowed around it. "You're missing the point."

"Which is?"

"We don't even know each other."

He reached for her. "We can fix that soon enough."

"By having sex?"

His eyes narrowed before his mouth relaxed into a smile that took her breath away. "Well, I'm not usually a first-date kind of guy, but for you, I'm willing to be flexible."

She wasn't sure whether to laugh or slug him. "You're being obtuse."

"No, I'm confused." He rubbed the side of his face. "Although, on second thought, maybe I do understand. You enjoyed me kissing you. But you got cold feet when you realized I wanted that bra gone—"

"Do you like me, Brent?"

He looked taken aback. "What kind of question is that?"

"A perfectly legitimate one," she answered, feigning a calmness she didn't feel.

"You think I'm in the habit of making out with women I dislike?"

"I think you're attracted to me physically, but

you don't know me well enough to like me or not."

"That's not true."

"What do you know about me?"

He considered her for a long moment as if she were a meal he wanted to devour. "When I was inside Forrester's house, you came back for me even though you were terrified of the fire. And when we found McKenna, you suggested he seek out the paramedics. So I'd say, based on your actions, I like you fine.

"And I'm attracted to you," he continued. "In fact, I'd like nothing more than to pick up where we left off. But I don't put the moves on a woman who isn't interested. So it's my turn to ask a question, Claire. Are you interested—or not?"

Of course, she was interested, and that was the problem. If he touched her again, she'd abandon all common sense for the pleasure she would find in his bed. And mixing it up with an agent, however temporarily, would be a huge mistake.

The solution was simple. Kill his interest in her. "Nothing's changed since this morning. I'm still a psychologist."

He had the audacity to shrug. "Which is why you're talking this whole thing to death instead of admitting you want me."

She gritted her teeth. "You're project-ing—"

He laughed low in his throat. "If you think resorting to shrink lingo will put me off, you're wrong. You kissed me back."

"You surprised me."

"For a few seconds," he conceded. "After that, you were enjoying yourself. A lot."

She hated the smugness of his tone, hated even more that the words he spoke were true.

"So what if I enjoyed kissing you? That doesn't mean… You're practically a stranger."

"We can discuss our favorite foods and movies later. For now, stop analyzing and go with the flow."

She folded her arms. "As far as I'm concerned, the flow has stopped."

He looked disappointed, but philosophical. "There's always next time."

"There won't be a next time," she said, in an effort to convince herself as much as him. "We have to stick together until Forrester is apprehended. Then we go our separate ways."

He frowned, as if tired of arguing with her.

She tucked her tank top into her jeans. "I'm sorry I gave you mixed messages. I just don't want to act on an impulse that I'll regret afterward."

But as she left the room, a voice inside taunted

her with a different possibility—that she might later regret *not* acting on the impulse.

She fervently hoped that voice was wrong.

C<small>LAIRE WAS RIGHT</small>, Brent decided. Sleeping together would make an already complicated situation even more so. He should be grateful her common sense had nixed their passion. But he wasn't. Her exotic taste still lingered on his lips, her sweet fragrance still filled his nostrils and her excited gasp still rang in his ears. If she hadn't left the room, he'd have been hard pressed to keep his hands to himself. Because despite the arguments she'd made, he was sure he could make her forget logic and respond to him.

He cursed softly. He needed to stop thinking about her and start thinking about Forrester.

Firing up his laptop, he opened the file containing the scanned material from the house.

But after twenty minutes of reviewing bank statements, he pushed back from the table in disgust. If Forrester had acquired illegal funds, he wasn't stupid enough to deposit them into this account. So where were they?

Maybe he'd call Pete to brainstorm—

Except his buddy wasn't available to take his call. Ever.

Dammit, Pete. Why did you have to get yourself killed?

He sucked in a breath, braced himself for the onslaught of familiar questions. Why hadn't Pete waited for him to return from training in Quantico so they could go together? Or secured other backup? Why had a guy, whose Bureau nickname was the Bloodhound, failed to smell a setup at the Enbridge warehouse? Why had he—

Stop it.

He couldn't change what had happened. He

couldn't turn back time and reorder events the way he wanted to. He had to stop wishing, stop wondering, stop feeling.

Numb was the only way he could hold it together until Pete's killer received justice—a life sentence to rot in prison. And that sweet retribution would lessen his bitter loss.

Chapter Six

An hour later, Claire left her room and ventured into the kitchen. At first, she thought Brent was working on his laptop, but then she realized the screensaver was on, and he was staring into space.

Was he thinking about Forrester, mulling over leads to pursue? Or was he preoccupied with memories of the friend who had used the first aid kit that lay open on the table? She guessed it was Sanderson on his mind, and her heart went out to him. Brent gave the impression of being so strong it was easy to forget he'd sustained a terrible loss only two weeks ago. Did he have any family or friends he felt close enough to talk to? She suspected he hadn't opened up to anyone. He struck her as a loner, a man who would bury his pain, figuring it would cease to exist if he ignored it.

If only that were true.

In her experience, negative feelings that weren't acknowledged could turn corrosive, toxic. Her father's guilt had ripped him apart, destroyed his life. And she hadn't realized until it was too late that his failure to communicate had intensified his suffering.

Brent had saved her life. The least she could do was to offer him a sympathetic ear.

"How long had you known Sanderson?" she asked softly.

His eyes snapped into focus. "Why do you ask?"

"I want to get to know you better."

His lips thinned. "I remember saying we could discuss favorite foods and movies. I don't remember any mention of dead friends."

He was trying to shock her into silence, but there was too much at stake for her to give up. "I think the people we spend time with tell more about us than what we eat or watch."

He shrugged.

"Sometimes it helps to share your feelings—"

"—and sometimes it doesn't."

"How do you know? Have you tried to talk to anyone about them?"

"That's none of your business."

Damn, he was stubborn. He was also hurting. If she could only find the right words.

"On second thought," he said, "I guess that *is* your business. Pushing people to unload their personal baggage. Manipulating them into—"

"Insulting me won't take away your pain," she observed.

"The only pain here is the one you've become." He stood and moved away from the table.

"I don't mean to upset you. I just want to—"

"You just want to add me to the list of people you've psychoanalyzed." His lips twisted into a sneer. "Give it up, Claire. I won't ever bare my soul to you."

He went to the sink, splashed water over his face. Then he braced his hands on the counter and stared out the window.

Disappointed that he'd shut her down, she switched to a neutral topic. "Gene mentioned Forrester might have had inside help to get out of Ridsdale. Has the staff there been questioned?"

He nodded. "Gene sent agents to the hospital

to interview every employee. Nobody admitted to knowing anything."

No surprise there. "When did the interviews take place?"

"The night of his escape."

"At that point, Harris was alive."

"So?"

"You could use his murder as a reason to speak to them."

"But you don't believe Forrester killed him."

"It doesn't matter what I believe. It's what the person who helped him believes. Believing you're an accomplice to a murder would shake up most people."

Brent folded his arms over his chest, reluctant to admit that she had made a valid point. He would conduct the second round of interviews at Ridsdale himself. This time it made sense to take Claire with him. She was familiar with the facility and its operations, knew the rules and protocol. And although he didn't believe her professional training gave her any special insight, two sets of eyes and ears were better than one.

"We'll go tomorrow."

As she nodded her agreement, her blond curls fell over her shoulder. He fought a sudden urge to tangle his fingers in her hair. It would be soft, just like her lips. If he tugged her closer and nuzzled the corner of her mouth, maybe he could change her mind about kissing him again.

He tensed, his fingers itching to move.

But she would hardly welcome his touch after the way he had snapped at her. He hadn't intended to be mean. He just couldn't keep his emotions locked down if he talked about Pete.

He relaxed his fingers.

The trip to Ridsdale was important. Not only because it might result in a lead to Forrester, but because the less time he spent alone with Claire, the better.

THE STAFF MEMBERS at Ridsdale Psychiatric Hospital weren't happy about being interviewed again. They'd already told the FBI what they knew about the evening that Forrester had escaped. Being questioned again and by another agent suggested that one or more employees was suspected of lying—or at least withholding information. So Claire wasn't at all surprised by the interviewees' range of reactions—defensiveness, belligerence, confusion and resignation. Unfortunately, those differing attitudes made it tricky to spot deceit.

Brent had started the second round of interviews with the employees identified by the original investigators as top suspects. Five had been flagged either because of their conduct during the initial questioning or the results of the subsequent background check.

He turned to Maria Gomez, a petite thirty-two-year-old nurse and mother of two young children, who was the last of the staff to be questioned.

"You have previously discussed the escape of a Ridsdale patient, Andy Forrester, with one of my colleagues."

"That's right."

Claire watched the woman's fingers twist together in her lap.

"I'm here today to ask if you've remembered anything else that might be pertinent to our investigation."

"No, I haven't."

"At the time Forrester was admitted, he hadn't committed any crimes. The person who

helped him escape might not have believed he
was dangerous."

The nurse's fingers twisted faster.

"He can be persuasive," Brent said. "It's possible he convinced someone that a mistake
had been made, that he shouldn't have been
confined."

Claire liked Brent's strategy. He was pro-
viding the woman with justification for her
actions—if she was, in fact, involved.

"It doesn't matter what you told the other
agent," he prodded. "All that matters is what
you tell me now."

"You think I was lying when I talked to that
other guy?"

Claire noted the tension in her shoulders, the
pallor of her skin. Were they signs of indigna-
tion or guilt?

"I think that you may have been worried
about the consequences," he allowed. "And

no one could have guessed that, once out, Forrester would kill one FBI agent and injure another."

Maria's gaze dropped to her lap, where her white knuckles stood out against her peach uniform. "Is that really true?"

He nodded. "He tried to kill Dr. Lamont and me, too. Whoever helped him get out of here could be charged as an accessory to those crimes unless he or she cooperates with the investigation."

She remained silent.

"If you have any idea where he is, you need to tell me. Before he hurts anybody else."

"I have nothing to say."

Brent's gaze grew steely. "It's just a matter of time until Forrester's caught. When he is, the identity of his accomplice will come to light."

Maria raised her chin. "I have to go now. My kids are waiting for me at the sitter's."

After the nurse left, Brent asked Claire, "What do you think? Did Forrester have inside help?"

"I can't imagine how he escaped otherwise. The security procedures are excellent."

But helping Forrester leave Ridsdale was a far cry from arson or murder. She didn't see any of the five she'd met today participating in that. Certainly not Maria Gomez. But something about the petite nurse had Claire's internal radar pinging. "I think Maria Gomez was involved."

Brent frowned. "My prime suspect is Wayne Bonsall."

"Why?"

Brent pointed to files he'd collected from the Bureau office. "The background info shows his charge cards are maxed out. Given his orderly's wages, it'll take him years to pay them off."

"You think Forrester bribed him?"

"Yeah, I do."

Bonsall's resentment over being paid less than the nurses had been evident early in the interview. So why was her intuition still pointing her in the nurse's direction?

"What happens next?" she asked.

"I'm going to recommend surveillance."

"For whom?"

"Wayne Bonsall…and Maria Gomez."

She could have sworn her heart skipped a beat. Damn, there was something about the man that got her worked up.

She shifted her gaze away from the sensual curve of his lips to the moss-green wall behind him. But her eyes rebelled, sliding back to study the man across from her, drawn to him by an invisible force that was stronger than her ability to resist it.

Sprawled in a chair, his body appeared lax, almost lazy, but she knew only too well the steely strength of the muscles that lay beneath his cotton shirt. She'd felt the power of those muscles when he'd lifted her through Forrester's office window. It wasn't just his physique she found tantalizing. Her mouth tingled with the memory of his kiss. Just the right amount of pressure, just the right amount of tongue. In fact, everything about it had been perfect. She wanted to clear the table of those files, push him down on top of it and have her way with him.

She clasped her damp hands together, told herself that her fantasy was wildly inappropriate. This was a hospital, for crying out loud.

Besides, did she really want to set herself up for heartache by becoming involved with a man who was emotionally distant and dismissive of her profession? Far better to disappoint her raging hormones now than have to live with hurtful memories later.

So she didn't jump Brent but waited patiently while he loaded files into a black case. Clearly, she was the only one whose thoughts had strayed to sex. His focus was on arranging surveillance and locating Forrester.

Or so she thought, until he asked, "How come you work mostly with federal agents?"

It was a question she'd been asked before, so she had a pat answer ready. "My dad worked for the Bureau, so I'm familiar with the pressures of the job and its impact on families."

His response was immediate and unequivocal. "Agents shouldn't have families."

"Why not?"

"The job requires one hundred percent commitment."

Did he really believe he had to sacrifice a personal life for the sake of his career? "Lots of agents have families."

"And lots of them end up as single parents and rarely see their kids."

"That doesn't have to happen."

"You can't tell me that divorces aren't more common for us."

She hesitated, loath to concede the point but knowing she had to. "It's true that certain professions—"

"—law enforcement, the military—" he supplied helpfully.

"—have higher rates of divorce than the general population," she persevered. "But that doesn't mean people in those careers should avoid getting married or forming close attachments. In fact, the opposite is true. The extraordinary demands of the job mean they need more, not less, support." Although she spoke in general terms, her thoughts centered on one man. Her father. He had had the support of a loving family but had still come to feel adrift, disassociated, alone. Her desire to be a psychologist had sprung from wanting to understand how depression had taken hold and dragged him into a downward spiral of despair.

Brent leaned back in his chair. "I'm not the only agent who thinks a family is a bad idea."

She forced her thoughts from the past to the present. "You're obviously not talking about Gene. He's been married for a long time and has three kids. So I'm guessing it was your friend, Pete Sanderson, who shared your view."

Brent frowned. "As a matter of fact, he did. Although he didn't start off that way. He married his college sweetheart the year after he joined the Bureau."

"And divorced a short time later, right?" Such an experience would explain his negative view.

"He told me the breakup of his marriage hurt him a hundred times more than any injury he got in the field."

"So you've decided not to risk it."

His eyes narrowed. "I only take calculated risks. There's no way to figure out the chances of a marriage lasting."

True. Marriage wasn't a logical decision reached by the brain. It was a leap of faith taken by the heart in love. She hoped to take that leap herself someday. "Did you always think this way?"

"I was engaged once," he admitted. "After I was accepted at the Bureau, I left for my sixteen weeks of training at the Academy. When

I came home, I found Sylvia, my fiancée, pregnant with another guy's baby."

He was talking dispassionately, but Claire suspected that betrayal was the reason he had no interest in a close relationship. Her heart went out to him for the hurt he'd suffered and evidently not recovered from. "I'm sorry, Brent."

"It's ancient history," he said, with a shrug.

Their conversation had been enlightening— and disappointing. For an agent as driven as Brent, his job would come first and last. A woman would never mean more to him than a temporary diversion.

No matter how insistently her hormones clamored, she mustn't indulge them.

Chapter Seven

Brent rubbed the back of his neck in frustration. Two days had passed since the trip to Ridsdale, and neither suspect under surveillance had made contact with Forrester. When Brent's cell phone rang, he answered it immediately, hoping for a break in the investigation.

"We found the dealer who sold the Trans Am to Forrester," Gene said. "His name is Fergus Lyons, and he remembers our suspect paid eighty thousand cash for the car. And get this. Forrester asked him to keep his eyes open for a sixty-five Cobra Roadster in mint condition."

"Where the hell is he getting the cash?" Brent asked.

"No leads on that yet."

"Any luck finding the Trans Am?"

"Langdon is contacting local garages in case it's being repaired."

"If nothing turns up there, tell him to widen the search to storage units."

"Anything else?"

"I found a sales slip for the laptop Forrester bought in the spring, but I didn't see it at his house." He glanced out the window at the lake shimmering in sunlight.

"It wasn't among his belongings when he was admitted to Ridsdale."

"Great. So now we're looking for his car *and* his laptop."

"I'll be in touch," Gene said.

Brent closed his phone, his gaze still on the view outside. A boat bearing two men with fishing poles chugged past the dock.

That should be Pete and me.

The thought hit hard—a sucker punch to the gut. Sanderson was dead while his killer roamed free. The wrongness of the situation seared like acid. He needed to know what was being done to catch Sanderson's killer. And Ian Alston, an investigator with the team, owed him a favor.

A PHONE CALL, a quick trip to Cincinnati and Brent had a flash drive containing all the pertinent info on the investigation. As he waited for his laptop to boot up, Pete's image came to mind. The blue eyes that had danced when he hooked a big one. The wide mouth that had belted out country tunes off-key. The strong arms that had carried him to safety after he'd been stabbed… Oh, God.

He sucked in a breath, waited for the pain to dull. Then he plugged in the flash drive, opened the first file and began reading.

He already knew the basics. Sanderson's body had been discovered at 11:30 p.m. at the Enbridge warehouse located at 15 Duke Street. Cause of death: the second of two bullets he'd taken in the chest.

A review of Sanderson's PDA indicated a meeting at 9:00 p.m. with one of his snitches, Marty Adey, who claimed he hadn't set foot in the warehouse. He'd received one thousand dollars to act as a go-between for a third party. His alibi for the time period was solid; he had been picked up for DUI at eight and spent the night in jail. Adey had spent half of the money he'd been paid, but the remaining bills had been confiscated as evidence and dusted for fingerprints. None matched the Bureau's database of felons.

The next file was a photo of Sanderson's naked body lying on a metal table, awaiting autopsy. He refused to let himself look away, refused to spare himself the hurt of seeing his friend that way. Because he knew Sanderson had endured an agony a thousand times worse when those bullets had drilled into his chest.

A horrified gasp had him pivoting around in his chair.

"That's your friend, Pete Sanderson, isn't it?" Claire asked from the doorway.

He closed his laptop, letting her draw her own conclusion.

She approached slowly as if she knew she was intruding but couldn't stop herself. "Has a suspect been identified yet?"

He avoided looking her in the eye. "Nope."

"This must be so frustrating for you."

He heard compassion in her voice and had the sudden urge to go to her, bury his face in her hair, breathe in her scent. She would be surprised, even astounded, but he was pretty sure she wouldn't deny him the comfort he craved.

He steeled himself against the impulse. *Numb is the only way to hold it together.*

"Investigations take time." A stock phrase used at the Bureau, but the words tasted like ashes in his mouth.

She came farther into the room, her hands shoved in her jean pockets. "You'd like to help with it, wouldn't you?"

"That's against the rules," he mocked.

"Because you and Pete were friends." She leaned a hip against the counter. "I understand the reasoning, but it doesn't seem fair, somehow."

"It *isn't* fair."

"But you'll abide by the rules, right?"

That was his cue to stop talking. If she guessed he had unauthorized access to the case files, she'd feel obligated to warn him of the consequences—disciplinary action courtesy of the review board.

His cell phone rang, a welcome interruption. He glanced at the caller ID display. "It's Gene."

She moved away. "We'll continue this conversation later."

Oh no, we won't.

He flipped open his phone. "What have you got, Gene?"

"A guy at U Lock It saw a white Trans Am being driven into one of his units a few weeks ago. Our agent showed him a photo of Forrester and confirmed that he's renting the unit. I should have a search warrant signed off soon."

Brent straightened as a fresh rush of adrenaline pumped through his system. "I want to be on-site when it's opened."

"You can take the warrant to the storage facility. Mickey Langdon is watching the unit."

Brent disconnected and pocketed his phone.

Sanderson's files would have to wait. Because no matter how badly he wanted to solve his friend's murder, his first priority was to locate Forrester and stop him from killing again.

THE U LOCK IT storage facility sprawled over a sizable stretch of industrial park just west of the city. Claire leaned forward in her seat, checking for the main entrance.

"Turn there," she said, pointing to the next driveway.

Brent spun the wheel to the right. "There's supposed to be an agent waiting for us."

A prefabricated office structure faced a long row of gray storage units with eight-foot-high blue garage doors. Brent flashed his headlights twice, then parked adjacent to unit 5.

A man with a crew cut and a bodybuilder physique materialized from the side of the building. He loped over to the car and pressed his credentials against the glass.

Brent lowered his window. "Good to meet you, Langdon."

"Likewise." The agent switched his gaze to the passenger seat. "Hey, Claire. You trade in your couch for fieldwork?"

She smiled at his teasing remark. Last November, Mickey Langdon had found it hard to get out of bed, much less tease anyone. He had come to her after his twin brother had died of lung cancer. The disease ran rampant in the Langdon clan, and Mickey was obsessed with the idea that his own death was imminent.

After several sessions, she managed to convince him to go to his doctor, who ordered a complete medical workup and prescribed the patch to help him quit smoking. Mickey had called her afterward to say all tests had come back normal, and he was cigarette-free for the first time since high school. He took Zoloft for depression but was fully functional.

"Brent brought the search warrant," she said, shoving up the sleeves of her cardigan sweater.

"He brought more than that," Mickey replied. "He brought my favorite psychologist. Thanks to you, I'm back at work."

"Speaking of work—" Brent began.

"I'll talk to the manager." Mickey jogged toward the office building.

Brent turned to her. "You have a fan."

She smiled. "Not everybody at the Bureau tries to avoid me."

He hooked his thumbs over the steering wheel, his blue shirt rippling like water over his chest. "Oh, I believe that."

She detected an edge in his tone. "You think guys like Mickey want something other than counseling when they come to see me, don't you?"

His eyes narrowed. "I think some people can't resist dumping their problems onto others."

"But you're an island."

His smile sent an arrow of awareness straight through her. "You got that right, doc."

A door banged in the distance. A tall, lanky man crossed the pavement toward them.

Brent left the car, and Claire heard Mickey introduce him to Kevin Curtis.

Brent held out the search warrant. "We're authorized to search unit number five."

Curtis glanced at the document. "I've never seen one of these before, but it looks official."

"Mr. Curtis just told me that he saw a guy hanging around here early this morning," Mickey said.

"Forrester?" Brent asked.

Claire felt her stomach knot.

"I can't be sure," Curtis said. "He had his back to the office. When I came outside, he got in his car and took off like a bat out of hell."

"Did you notice the make and model of the vehicle he was driving?" Mickey asked.

"Nah, I was barely awake. It wasn't the Trans Am, that I do know."

Brent turned toward the unit. "We'd like to get started."

"How long is this going to take?" Curtis asked, retrieving a key from his pocket.

"Depends on what's in there."

"Well, if you think you might be a while, you need to move your car. I got three moving vans coming to unload this afternoon, and they can't do it with you parked there."

"Where to?" Brent asked, opening the driver's door of the Mustang.

Curtis pointed. "Down at the end should be okay."

Brent pulled around and reversed into the space Curtis had indicated.

"You might as well wait here," he told Claire. "I can keep an eye on both you and the exterior of the building while Langdon does the first sweep of the unit."

Brent headed out, and she caught herself admiring the quick, powerful movements of his legs. Damn, even the man's walk was sexy.

She glanced away, settled deeper into the Mustang's leather seat.

A moment later, a loud boom shook the car.

She bolted upright. A dark form lay prone on the asphalt twenty feet from the office.

Brent.

Flinging open the door, she raced toward him, sucking in a breath only when she saw him stir. He was on his feet by the time she got to his side, and he was—thank God—seemingly uninjured. Relief flooded through her so strongly, she nearly sank to her knees.

A gut-wrenching scream came from the storage units.

She turned her head, then gasped in horror. The blast had blown off Mickey's right hand. Blood sprayed from the severed limb onto the asphalt.

The manager of the facility lay sprawled a few feet away. There was no blood, but his leg was bent at an awkward angle, probably broken. He appeared to be unconscious.

"Claire!" Brent yelled.

She looked toward him mutely.

"Call nine-one-one." He tossed his cell phone to her.

She caught it and started punching in the numbers as he raced toward the men.

By the time she'd completed the call and joined him, Brent had cinched his belt around Mickey's forearm. "Easy, man. Help's on the way."

Claire stripped off her sweater and used it to staunch the gaping wound. Her stomach churned as the blood soaked through, turning the garment and her hands crimson. The metallic smell of blood flooded her nose, and it took a supreme act of willpower not to gag.

"Why?" the wounded agent panted.

"Good question," Brent said grimly, glancing toward the smoking hole in the unit.

"Search it…before the cops come."

"I'm not leaving you." Brent checked under

the sweater, testing the belt to ensure it was choking off the blood flow.

Mickey shoved at him weakly with his remaining hand. "Claire…can stay."

She made shushing noises as she stroked his forehead. "I'm here, Mickey. Don't try to talk."

His head thrashed from side to side. "Go. Hurry."

She glanced at Brent, sick with worry. "I think you'd better go. He won't rest until you do."

Brent began to argue, but one look at his colleague's pleading eyes had him rising to his feet. "I'll be right back."

She watched, feeling strangely bereft as he set off for the damaged unit.

Mickey moaned in pain. "Always figured… I'd die from the big C."

"You're not going to die," she said fiercely. "You're a tough hombre."

"Hurts." He spoke through clenched teeth.

"You'll get something for the pain, just as soon as the ambulance arrives."

His torso jerked off the pavement suddenly.

She cradled him in her arms. "Lie still, Mickey. Please."

He didn't respond, and she realized it was because he was no longer conscious. Looking at his closed eyes, slack mouth and gray skin, she experienced a helplessness that she'd never known before. He was one of the few agents who had ever appreciated her assistance, and he was counting on her. She would *not* fail him.

"Where's the damn ambulance?" she yelled in frustration.

She turned her head, hoping to see Brent on

his way back to them, but he was still inside the storage unit.

She stared intently at its jagged, blackened entrance, her anxiety escalating. Surely, she should be able to catch a glimpse of his pale T-shirt or hear him moving around in there.

What if another bomb had been hidden inside? What if Brent were attempting to disarm it?

Scared and covered in blood, she fought the urge to scream.

Chapter Eight

Brent hurried through the debris that littered Forrester's rented storage unit, knowing that he had only minutes to search.

When the cops arrived, they'd secure the crime scene, and no one would be permitted inside until the CSI guys had completed their painstaking evidence-gathering process. Then more time would be wasted while the Bureau and the local police department wrangled over jurisdiction.

The acrid smell of smoke and chemicals invaded his nostrils and burned his eyes.

The Trans Am stood directly ahead of him, its trunk empty and cleaved in two by a blue metal projectile that had once been part of the storage unit door. The fender looked like crumpled aluminum foil. All the windows had shattered, dusting the vehicle with a layer of sparkling crystals.

He edged around the side of the car. The driver's door hung ajar from the force of the explosion.

Tugging on his driving gloves, he proceeded to search the interior. The glove compartment contained a Trans Am owner's manual and a flashlight. He thumbed through the manual, then unscrewed the top section of the flashlight, removed the batteries and peered inside the empty cylinder.

Next, he flipped down both sun visors and checked the pockets on the driver and passenger doors. Using the flashlight, he went over the front seats and carpet, trying not to disturb the glass shards while he examined every damn inch. Then he moved to the backseat and repeated his search.

Nothing.

That left the interior of the roof. His fingers ran back and forth, feeling for any irregularity in the fabric. After several passes, he detected a raised section near the overhead light. He traced the shape with his fingers, then blasted the area with the flashlight. The fabric had been neatly sliced and something inserted. He coaxed the thin, ragged-edged item from its hiding place.

A key.

Too small for a vehicle or door lock, it seemed about the right size for a locker or trunk. He exited the car, trying to remember if he'd seen anything the key might fit at Forrester's house.

The flashlight lit up the back wall of the storage unit, revealing a multidrawer metal cabinet. He went over and tugged on the top drawer. When it wouldn't open, he tried the key, which quickly released the locking mechanism. The cabinet drawers held numerous automotive tools.

Why would Forrester bother to secure them separately when he had a locked storage unit?

After extracting all five drawers from the cabinet frame, Brent knelt down, reached inside and felt along the back and both sides. Then, remembering the car, he touched the top of the cabinet. His hand made contact with a half-inch ridge in the shape of a square. The flashlight showed a CD case taped to the underside.

As he removed the case, the ripping sound was followed by the muted wail of emergency sirens. He pocketed the CD and strode out of the storage unit.

"How's he doing?" he called out, crossing the parking lot.

"Not good," Claire said, strain evident in her face. "He passed out a few minutes ago, and his color's been getting worse ever since. Those sirens had better be his ambulance."

When she touched the side of Langdon's neck for his pulse, Brent saw her hands were shaking and bloodstained. "I'm sorry you had to deal with this."

She glanced up, squinting in the bright sunshine. "Did you find anything?"

"An unlabeled CD."

As the sound of the sirens grew louder, he added quickly, "My gut tells me it's important."

An ambulance swung onto the U Lock It

property and drove up the laneway toward them, followed closely by a police cruiser.

"Let's hope your gut is right," she said.

THE PASSWORD protecting the unmarked CD was a clear sign to Brent that Forrester didn't want others accessing it. He made attempt after attempt to type the right combination of letters and numbers in the password box. He tried the man's birth date, his Social Security number and his employee number. Then his middle name, his mother's maiden name and all of the names listed in his address book. Within an hour, he was grinding his molars. The Bureau's tech guys had more practice unlocking protected files than he did, but it would take too long to go through official channels.

After another fifteen minutes, he was out of ideas—and caffeine.

Claire wandered into the kitchen as the coffee finished brewing. He poured two mugs and handed her one.

"Thanks." She lifted the cup to her lips and sipped. "I've never had this much free time. I feel restless."

"You could take the canoe out. Or go for a swim." An image popped into his head of Claire wearing a skimpy bikini, her curves covered by only scraps of material, her skin soft and bare—

He gulped down the hot coffee so fast his throat burned.

She strolled to the window, oblivious to the fantasy torturing him. "Anything creepy in the lake?"

He tried to settle himself down, but his voice came out hoarse. "Nothing but minnows near the shore. The last few days have been sunny so it should have warmed up a little."

She smiled. "Cold water doesn't bother me."

It didn't bother him, either. In fact, his body temperature could use lowering. But taking a dip in the lake with Claire wouldn't have the desired effect. It would only increase his desire for her.

"Do you want to join me?" she asked.

Of course he did. But until he cracked the password, he had no business doing—or thinking about—anything else.

He returned to the couch. "I'm still working on the CD from Forrester's car."

Her smile faded. "Of course."

He knew his words had reminded her of the incident at the storage unit, and he regretted that. Claire had made several calls to the hospital to check on Mickey's condition but hadn't been given much information.

He turned back to the computer on the coffee table.

What should he try next? Forrester's driver's license number? He checked the info in the file Lisa had downloaded at the office, then entered the necessary keystrokes.

Access denied.

"How long have you been at that?" Claire asked.

"Too long," he muttered.

"What are you trying to do?"

Brent rubbed the back of his neck. "Figure out his password. Most people pick something easy to remember."

"I use my zip code," she admitted.

"If Forrester had, I'd have cracked the sucker in ten minutes."

He leaned back, rolling his shoulders to work out the kinks. "Why don't you take a stab at it?"

Her eyes widened. "Me?"

He'd spoken on impulse but now decided

that getting her involved wasn't a bad idea. "Hey, you've spent more time with this guy than I have."

"That doesn't mean I can help."

"Well, I'm out of ideas. It's your turn to get frustrated."

She sat beside him. "Forrester's passion is classic cars. Have you tried the Trans Am's license plate number?"

"Puh-lease," he said, rolling his eyes.

"Sorry. What about the year of the car?"

"It's worth a shot." He typed in "1969," hit Enter and checked the screen.

Access denied.

He was beginning to hate those words.

"Forrester has a nickname for his car that he mentioned during one of our sessions. It's Beauty."

Brent typed in the six letters, just to humor her.

The empty password box disappeared, and

the image of a Trans Am loaded onto the screen. He was in.

Beauty, indeed.

Claire peered over his shoulder. "Hey, it worked. Are you happy?"

He was *very* happy. And damn grateful she hadn't taken his suggestion and gone swimming. He leaned over and pressed his mouth against hers.

What started as a kiss of gratitude quickly became more. As soon as his lips made contact, he forgot everything but how much he wanted her. He kissed her again, not caring that there were reasons he shouldn't. He'd been holding back too long, stifling urges that were demanding to be acted on.

She sighed and kissed him back.

Last time, he'd misjudged her comfort zone by moving too fast. He wouldn't make that mistake again. It wasn't a damn race, it was an experience to be savored. *She* was an experience to be savored. And he intended to show her he understood that.

He had to be doing something right because Claire kept up with him, kiss for kiss. Then she wrapped her arms around him. As her fingertips massaged his heated flesh through his shirt, he moaned in pleasure.

He was damn well going to make her moan, too.

He nibbled a trail of kisses along her jaw, then down her neck to her collarbone, marveling at the softness of her skin and her tantalizing fragrance. Near the swell of her breast, he slowed, not wanting to assume too much, but she threaded her fingers through his hair and urged him to move lower. Her breathing quickened in anticipation, and his heartbeat did the same.

She was beautiful, vibrant and passionate.

And so very responsive to his caresses. Her nipples pebbled under her tank top, and she strained against his body so that he hardened until he ached.

His lips nuzzled her breast through the thin cotton. He slid a hand under her top and stroked her stomach.

It's wrong to be making out with Claire while Sanderson's killer is on the loose.

He sucked in a breath and pressed his hot face against her neck. Although he desperately wanted to keep touching Claire, the voice inside his head couldn't be ignored. He had more important priorities than to satisfy his desires.

Before he could change his mind, he moved away.

Claire swayed in her seat, her mouth swollen from his kisses, her skin flushed with excitement.

"Thanks for cracking the code," he said, keenly aware that his words sounded brusque and impersonal. "I have to get back to work now."

She looked away, but not before he saw the hurt and confusion in her eyes.

Disgust lodged in his stomach. He shouldn't have touched her, shouldn't have allowed himself to forget—even for a moment—that his energies had to be directed elsewhere. She might not appreciate it now, but he'd done her a favor by stopping. He couldn't give her the attention she deserved—even in the short term—and he'd never been a long-term kind of guy.

From this point on, he had to focus solely on catching Forrester and identifying Sanderson's killer.

Claire gripped the sides of her chair, struggling for composure. The last time she'd felt like this, she'd been riding a friend's horse when it had spooked and thrown her to the ground. Then as now, having the breath knocked out of her wasn't the worst part. It was the sense of complete disorientation.

Why had Brent withdrawn from her just when things were getting interesting? To pay her back for shying away from intimacy before? Or had he decided making love to her would be a mistake? Both possibilities upset her. She'd finally accepted their relationship for what it was: an exciting, sexually-charged connection. That fell short of all that she wanted, but maybe it would grow into more if she took a chance.

Apparently, he wasn't going to give them that chance.

Outside, the sun was setting, painting the lake and beach a glittering gold. Despite the turmoil in her life, she couldn't remember a more peaceful setting. No wonder Brent and

Pete had enjoyed coming here. Maybe if her father had had such a place to unwind, things would have turned out differently.

The old ache rose up, but she ruthlessly pushed it back down. The past was done, and no amount of speculation could change it.

Even though a relationship between her and Brent was a no-starter, she was worried about him. He had so much on his mind that he could delay coming to terms with his loss. But eventually there would be a lull, and then the pain and grief would strike him like a tidal wave. She hoped, when the time came, he had somebody to call on for support.

Too bad he wouldn't allow that *somebody* to be her.

UNABLE TO SLEEP, Brent lay in the darkness, his mind jumping from one thought to another. The discovery of Forrester's password had allowed him to open the CD's files, but then he'd hit a wall. The contents were strings of letters and numbers whose meaning eluded him.

What he wished would elude him was his awareness of Claire. It didn't matter how often he told himself to ignore her, he simply could not shut her out. Every move she made, every look she sent his way, fed his attraction to her.

He wanted to taste her and touch her again— not just her lips, but every inch of her. It was an urge he'd been feeling since they'd met, an urge that was harder to resist with every minute they spent together. Today, she had responded with heat and passion…until he'd shoved her away.

That seemed like such a stupid, hurtful move now.

He didn't want her spending the night alone next door. He didn't want a wall separating them. He wanted them to be in the same room, in the same bed, where he'd soon take away her hurt and make her feel like the most desirable woman in the world.

Stop it.

He'd lost sight of his assignment. He was supposed to protect her, not lust after her. Besides, she wouldn't be content with a fling, and he couldn't offer her anything more.

His stomach grumbled, and he decided a quick trip to the fridge might help him sleep. He padded barefoot through the hall but stopped when he reached the living room. Moonlight streamed through the window, showcasing a blanketed form huddled in a chair. Evidently, Claire couldn't sleep, either.

He debated beating a retreat, but that was a coward's way. He had to face her and tell her she hadn't done anything wrong earlier. He just wasn't the right man for her.

As he advanced into the room, only the soft curls of her hair and pale oval of her face were visible above the blanket.

"How long have you been awake?" he asked.

"An hour," she admitted. "I can't stop thinking about Mickey. One minute, he was standing there, perfectly fine. The next…" She pressed her fingers to her mouth. "I wish they'd let me ride in the ambulance with him."

"He wouldn't have known you were there," Brent pointed out. "And once he reached the hospital, the doctors would've sent you away while they worked on him."

"I know you're right." She let out a weary sigh. "I just wish I knew how he's doing. The hospital won't tell me much."

"Gene called after you went to bed," Brent said. "Langdon's scheduled for surgery the day after tomorrow."

"Why?"

"He has to have a few inches of bone removed so the skin can cover the stump."

She shivered, and drew the blanket more tightly around her. "Poor Mickey."

"His doctor said the prognosis is good. There's no sign of infection, and he should be out of surgery in a few hours."

"Thanks for telling me," she said, her lips curving softly.

Maybe this was his chance to make amends. "Do you want to go to the hospital tomorrow? You could visit with him, maybe meet his fiancée. Gene said she wants to thank you in person for calling the ambulance and staying with him until it arrived."

Her eyes glowed in the moonlight. "Thanks, I'd like that."

Her gratitude sent a rush of warmth through him. Actually, her company often had that effect on him—and not only when he was kissing her.

The thought brought him up short. The late hour was probably to blame, but even so he shouldn't be thinking along those lines. It didn't matter what he felt when he was around Claire. It only mattered that he kept her safe until Forrester was in custody.

"We'll go after breakfast," he said.

Before Claire could respond, the ring of his cell phone intruded.

He glanced at the illuminated display, frowning when it showed Gene's home number. He flipped it open. "What's up?"

"It's Langdon," Gene said. "There was a blood clot."

He swore softly. A blood clot could mean a dozen different things—none of them good. "How is he?"

"He died an hour ago."

Chapter Nine

The next morning Brent was up early, having spent the night tossing and turning. Langdon had died because Forrester hadn't wanted anybody to discover the CD. What made the damn thing worth killing for?

He opened the first file and stared at the contents. The letters and numbers had to be a code. But how could he decipher it without knowing the key?

His cell phone rang. It was Ian Alston, the agent who had given him the flash drive. "You were right to question that ballistics report.

The two slugs that were tested weren't the ones that came out of Sanderson."

"How the hell could that happen?"

"Somebody at the lab screwed up."

"So the team has spent weeks searching for the wrong caliber gun?"

"Afraid so."

He swore. "Let me know when the new results are available."

"You got it."

"Has anybody figured out who No Neck is?" The nickname had shown up on Sanderson's PDA.

"He was a homeless junkie," Ian said.

"Was?"

"The guy died last week. Massive organ failure."

Brent crossed out his "interview pending" notation.

"There's something else you should know,"

Ian said. "During the Eddie Hola investigation, Sanderson ran surveillance on a guy named David Cantrell. Sanderson caught Cantrell cheating on his wife on film."

"How is that relevant?"

"Cantrell received copies of Sanderson's photos in mid-April. Soon afterward, he withdrew seventy-five thousand dollars from his bank."

"What are you saying? That Sanderson was blackmailing him?" The idea was ludicrous.

"Lots of agents had access to the Hola files," Ian said in a conciliatory tone.

"Has anyone talked to Cantrell?"

"He's dead. Shot at close range. The money's missing. A team is coming from the Oklahoma office to investigate."

"Who's under suspicion?"

"I was given a gag order on the names, but I think you can guess one of them."

"Forrester." The agent who had paid eighty thousand cash for the Trans Am. The agent who had already killed a colleague and wounded another.

"I'll call if I hear anything else," Ian said, and disconnected.

Brent returned to staring at his laptop screen. Could the strings of gibberish relate to payoff amounts? Partway down his laptop screen, he saw one ending with 75. Ian had said that Cantrell had been blackmailed for that amount.

Could this be the key he had been looking for?

He wrote "David Cantrell" on a sheet of paper, circling the two *D*s, two *A*s and two *L*s. Next he copied the letters from the string. NKFSNMKXDBOVV. The presence of two *N*s, two *K*s and two *V*s confirmed his suspicion. Forrester had transcribed Cantrell's name by replacing the D with an N, the A with a K, and so on.

He spent the next ten minutes unscrambling the names in the files. Then he came to one that looked familiar. Jim Sharratt. How did he know that name? It took him an hour to locate the name buried in a report. Sharratt and Sanderson had met for an hour in late May.

Why would a name on Forrester's CD match with someone Sanderson had contacted shortly before his murder?

He phoned Ian. "I need you to run the name Jim Sharratt through our databases."

Ian checked the spelling, and Brent stayed on the line while the other man completed the search.

"Okay, here's what I found," Ian said. "Last year, the Bureau was tracking visitors to child-porn Web sites. Sharratt was on the list."

"What happened?"

"Only those suspected of direct involvement with minors were arrested. Sharratt wasn't one of them."

"Who were the investigators?"

There was a short pause and the sound of keystrokes. "Heydon, Mills and Forrester."

No surprise there. "What kind of background info do we have on Sharratt?"

"Born in 1934," Ian said. "U.S. citizen. Owned a dozen successful companies but retired a few years ago. He's worth megabucks and had a squeaky clean record prior to the Internet porn operation."

Internet Porn Operation.

IPO.

Brent exhaled in a rush as Forrester's cryptic remark finally made sense. "Thanks," he muttered, and hung up.

A rich old man like Sharratt could afford to pay to bury his indiscretions. Had Forrester accepted money to keep him from being charged? Then there was Sanderson's meeting with Sharratt. How had that come about? Had the Bloodhound uncovered new information about the case and questioned him? To stop further digging, Sharratt could have arranged for Sanderson to be killed.

Brent rolled his shoulders, trying to work out the aches in his tight muscles. Conjecture was only a starting point. What he needed was evidence.

As he was shutting down his laptop, Claire appeared. "Any progress?" she asked.

"Yes, but first I want to tell you that I made a bad decision yesterday. I should have gone with Langdon to open the unit."

She looked horrified. "Why?"

"I might have noticed the lock had been tampered with." Then he could have stopped Langdon, and the guy would still be alive.

"But if you'd missed it, the explosion could have killed you, too."

She had a point. And if he died, he couldn't protect her from Forrester.

"It just doesn't make sense to me," she said.

"What? Mickey's death?"

"No, the bomb."

"Looks cut-and-dried to me. Forrester didn't want anybody to find the CD."

"Then why not choose a different hiding place for it?" She moved to sit on the couch. "According to his neighbors, that car was Forrester's pride and joy. Why would he risk destroying it? Especially when he paid a small fortune for it?"

"Okay, maybe the CD wasn't his only concern," Brent said. "Maybe he couldn't tolerate others gaining access to his Trans Am. So he rigged the unit to explode if it was opened."

"That's a really extreme thing to do."

"Fits with his other actions. Arson. Murder—"

"We can't prove he did anything except escape from Ridsdale," she pointed out.

"He's the only logical suspect." Claire's reluctance to accept Forrester's guilt irked him—as did the agent's skill at covering his tracks. "This time he got sloppy. The bomb squad reported there was enough explosive material to blow up the whole storage facility and a chunk of the parking lot, but the bomb wasn't properly rigged."

"Does Forrester have explosives experience?"

"Yes, he took special training last year. But remember the manager said he saw someone take off when spotted. Maybe Forrester botched the job because he was rushed."

"Or maybe it wasn't Forrester. Maybe someone wanted to kill him and got Mickey instead."

"That theory is a tough sell without corroborating evidence."

She was silent for a long moment. "You said you'd made some progress."

"I've figured out what IPO means," he said, "and I have a suspect for Sanderson's murder."

CLAIRE LISTENED intently as Brent explained the files on the CD related to suspects in an FBI Internet porn operation.

"Forrester was part of the IPO team," Brent added, "so he could have manipulated evidence to keep certain individuals from being prosecuted. I'm convinced he did that—for a payoff, of course."

"But how does that relate to Sanderson's murder?"

"One of the suspects, Jim Sharratt, met with Sanderson a few days before his murder."

"I still don't see the connection."

"Sanderson must have sniffed out something and contacted Sharratt. Alarmed by what Sanderson knew or might figure out, Sharratt had him killed."

"By Forrester?" she asked.

"That's a definite possibility. Forrester wouldn't have wanted his payoffs to be exposed." He pulled out his cell phone and punched in numbers.

"Who are you calling?"

"Sharratt."

"Wouldn't your colleagues have talked to him already?"

"I know they have," he agreed. "But the agents who interviewed him didn't know about his tie to the Internet porn case or Forrester."

He paced in front of the window, then spoke into the phone.

She heard him arrange to meet with Sharratt

the next day. And although she knew she should feel optimistic about this new development, Forrester's whereabouts were still unknown. That meant spending more days—and nights—with Brent.

She should be indifferent to his presence. He appeared to have no trouble shutting her out. Even if that changed, a relationship with him—no matter how exciting and thrilling—would ultimately lead to a dead end. Her awareness of these facts should act as armor, making her immune to his appeal.

And yet...

In spite of every argument her logical mind brought forward, she still wanted to be with him.

Explain that, doc.

JIM SHARRATT'S country estate included a sprawling stone house with elaborate gardens in the front and a swimming pool and tennis court around the back. Most people dreamed about retiring like this, Brent thought as he waited with Claire on the multitiered deck for their host to return with drinks. Still, most people would think twice about switching places with the guy if they knew he was an FBI suspect.

"I hope you don't mind cranberry juice," Sharratt said, as he emerged from the back of the house holding a tray. "I seem to be out of sodas."

"Cranberry juice is fine," Claire said, shading her eyes against the sun.

Sharratt set the drinks on a glass table, then lowered himself gingerly into a deck chair. "Ten years ago, I was strictly a Scotch man, but my doctor kept harping at me to take better care of my health. When I retired, I cut out booze, started eating right, and now

I play tennis five times a week, although my knees have been giving me trouble lately." He gave Brent an apologetic look. "But you didn't come to hear me grumble about the hassles of getting older. You came to talk to me about Pete Sanderson."

Brent nodded. "You told the other agents that you met with him May twenty-seventh."

"That's right. We shared ideas for reducing costs at the Last Resort Food Bank."

"Did you discuss anything else?"

Sharratt frowned. "Like what?"

"Like sex videos?"

Two bright spots appeared high on Sharratt's cheeks. "What are you talking about?"

Brent leaned forward and stabbed the table with his finger. "Do the words 'Internet porn' clarify matters for you?"

"No, they do not." Sharratt's tone was indignant, his gnarled hands gripping the arms of his deck chair.

"What about bribes? The ones you paid to keep from being prosecuted?"

"Bribes?" he repeated. "I don't know where you're getting your information, but you are dead wrong."

"Speaking of dead," Brent said, "who did you hire to kill Sanderson?"

Distress showed clearly on the older man's face. "Stop right there. I considered Pete Sanderson my friend."

"Well, I'm thinking any friendship you had with him ended when he threatened to expose your cozy arrangement with Forrester."

"I don't know anybody named Forrester." Sharratt rose to his feet with difficulty. "Get the hell out of here."

"Not just yet," Brent said, remaining in his seat. "I have more questions for you."

"I don't care how many more questions you have. I'm not talking to you again without my attorney present." He shuffled toward the patio door, looking noticeably older than when he'd come outside.

"It doesn't matter how many high-priced sharks you hire," Brent said, pushing back from the table. "The truth will come out."

Sharratt stopped just inside the opening to the house. "You say that as if you know the truth," he stated quietly. "But your wild accusations prove that you don't."

Brent straightened to his full height. "Well, you're in my sights now. I'll be gunning for you."

He left one of his cards on the table, weighted down by an empty tumbler. "If you decide to cooperate, call me. Because I won't stop until you're held accountable for every one of your crimes."

BRENT'S CELL PHONE rang two hours later, as they drove along the expressway heading out of the city.

It was Sharratt requesting another meeting immediately. Surprised by the man's urgent tone, Brent agreed and turned the Mustang around. This time, Sharratt didn't offer them drinks or make small talk. He appeared subdued, shaken. "I've changed my mind about talking to you."

"I'm listening," Brent said.

"My wife died last year."

Brent didn't see how the man's loss was relevant, but he remained silent, waiting.

"I didn't know what to do with myself. So my son got me a computer, set me up with an e-mail address and access to the Internet. Within a few days, I was getting all this porn stuff in my e-mail box."

Obviously, his son hadn't installed a decent

spam blocker. And for a man in his seventies, the concept of porn delivered to the home via personal computer was probably a strange—and titillating—experience.

"At first, I didn't even know what the subject lines meant, and I was shocked when I opened the first message. I immediately deleted it, of course, and so many others. But then…" His voice trailed off.

"But then what?"

Sharratt licked his lips. "I got curious."

Did the guy expect him to believe that he was only guilty of sneaking a few peeks? "So you checked out those smutty e-mails, right?"

"They came to me. I didn't go looking for this stuff." He glanced away. "At least, not at first."

Brent only raised his eyebrows.

Claire leaned forward, her expression sympathetic. "Then they invited you to check out some Web sites," she guessed.

He nodded. "And I did. Then I joined a chat room. I just wanted to look at some pictures, talk to some people."

"I doubt that would make you a suspect in an FBI investigation," Brent said.

Sharratt grimaced. "Well, I did a little more than that."

"Define 'more' for me."

"I ordered some movies."

"Kiddie porn," Brent said, unable to keep the disgust from his voice.

"I've never seen anything like it," the old man said. "Little girls being slapped around and forced to have sex." He shuddered.

"You understand that by ordering those movies, you encouraged the brutal exploitation of those children."

Sharratt flinched as if he'd been struck. When

he spoke again, his voice wavered. "I swear, I didn't know. In fact, I was so horrified by what I saw that I threw the movies in the trash.

"I wish I'd never got involved. And that's what I told Pete."

"Let's back up," Brent suggested. "Did you know you were a suspect in an Internet porn operation?"

"Nobody ever questioned me about it."

If Sharratt's story was true, Forrester wouldn't have needed to manipulate or expunge evidence from his file. The Bureau had targeted dangerous predators, not porn viewers. "Tell me about your meeting with Sanderson. Who set it up?"

"I did."

"Why?"

The man's gaze shifted to the thick area rug in the center of the living room floor. "I was scared."

"Of what?"

Sharratt lifted his head, his eyes filled with anxiety. "The man who threatened to kill my granddaughter if I refused to pay."

CLAIRE DARTED A LOOK at Brent, whose only outward sign of surprise was a flicker of his eyes. He must be one heck of a good poker player. But then, she already knew what a challenge it was to read him. He had alternately intrigued and frustrated her.

"Who's blackmailing you?" Brent demanded.

"I don't know. I've never seen him. I just leave the money where I'm told. Last time it was a hundred grand."

Brent looked at Claire.

She wondered if he was remembering her insistence that Forrester would need a big financial payoff to risk prison. A single payment of a hundred thousand dollars would certainly fit her definition of *big.*

"At first, he only threatened to expose my secret," Sharratt said. "I just couldn't bear losing the respect of my children, my friends and the members of my church. After several sleepless nights, I sold off some investments and paid, hoping that would be the end of it."

"But it wasn't," Brent stated flatly.

Sharratt grimaced. "He phoned two weeks later, demanding more money. When I balked at paying, he threatened to murder my grand-daughter. That's when I called Pete."

She saw a muscle in Brent's jaw clench before he asked, "Why Sanderson?"

"We've worked together on various chari-ties over the years. And I figured as an FBI agent, he'd know how to handle a situation like this."

"What did he advise?"

"He urged me to report everything, but I told him I couldn't risk the consequences and I begged him to respect my decision. Eventually he gave up trying to change my mind and asked if I knew why the blackmailer had picked me to shake down."

"And did you?"

"No, but I certainly wondered about it. So the second time he called, I asked him straight out. He just laughed and said, 'Research is the key.' I still have no idea what he meant, but Pete seemed shocked."

Claire shivered. Anybody who had spent time with Forrester would recognize that expression as one of his favorites.

Sharratt spoke in a sad monotone. "Pete said he had a hunch he wanted to follow up. That was the last I heard from him."

Claire shot Brent a quick look, but nothing

about him betrayed personal involvement. He had his feelings under complete control.

The old man passed a shaky hand over his face. "When the FBI contacted me, they said they were talking to everybody who had seen Pete recently. There was no mention of blackmail, so I figured no one knew what Pete and I had discussed. And I wasn't about to tell them."

Sharratt had no way of knowing his blackmailer was an FBI agent who would kill Sanderson rather than be forced to give up his "sweet deal."

"Did you pay the second time?" Brent asked.

"Yes, three weeks ago."

"Then what happened?"

"I heard nothing, and I hoped he'd forgotten about me. But he phoned today after you left, demanding another hundred thousand," Sharratt told them.

"When are you supposed to deliver the money?"

"He wanted it tomorrow, but I told him I couldn't liquidate my assets that fast, so he's given me three days to come up with the cash. He'll tell me the location later."

"How will you deliver it?" Brent said.

"He said to put the money in a black canvas bag. The bills are not to be sequentially numbered."

Forrester had made sure neither the money nor its container was unique enough to be identified at a later date.

Brent drummed his fingers on the arm of his chair, and Claire understood his frustration. Eventually, Forrester would be picked up. However, without Sharratt's positive ID of him or large amounts of unexplained cash, blackmail would be tough to prove. And the same was true of Sanderson's murder. To build a case against him, Brent needed evidence.

"If he contacts you again," Brent said, "call me immediately."

"You'll try to stop him?"

"I *will* stop him," he said, his jaw tight. "In the meantime, do whatever is necessary to get the money together. It's the bait we'll use to hook him."

Chapter Ten

Brent wasn't able to reach Gene until an hour after he and Claire had arrived back at the cabin. Sitting alone in the living room with the cell phone pressed against his ear, he decided it was time he was fully candid with his supervisor.

"There was a CD hidden in Forrester's vehicle," he told Gene when the other man finally came on the line. He quickly briefed him about decoding the information in the CD's files, matching a name to Sanderson's murder investigation and meeting with the blackmail victim.

When he was finished, Gene let out a low whistle. "As awful as this may sound, the Bloodhound's murder is finally beginning to make sense to me."

"Forrester must have figured out Pete knew about the blackmail scheme," Brent said. "He paid a snitch to set him up, and then he killed him."

Acid roiled in his stomach, and he shifted position, trying to ease the discomfort. Since the beginning, he'd been keeping Pete's loss at arms' length, telling himself he had to stay detached in order to solve the puzzle. But instead of feeling good that a crucial piece of the puzzle, motive, had slipped into place, he felt hollow, emptied out.

Gene cleared his throat. "Forrester's participation in the Bureau's Internet porn investigation means he had access to everything known about the suspects."

"That info helped him choose his targets."

"Nothing to stop him," Gene added.

"Until he picked the wrong one." The wrong one being Sharratt, longtime acquaintance of Pete Sanderson, who recognized Forrester's pet phrase.

"The blackmail drop is the best chance we have of apprehending Forrester," Gene said. "Let's meet tomorrow at nine to work on a plan."

"Sounds good."

"If the Bloodhound had lived a little longer," Gene added quietly, "he would have nailed Forrester's sorry hide to the wall."

"Damn right he would have."

"I'm sorry about Pete. I know I've said it before, but it always seems so damn inadequate."

Brent swallowed around the lump in his throat. Usually, he could come up with a glib response without breaking a sweat, but not right now.

After a lengthy pause, Gene continued, "I guess some things are just too big for words, huh?"

Brent cleared his throat and searched around for a way to lighten things up. "Don't let Claire catch you saying that. That woman believes talking can solve all the problems of the world."

"You should listen to her. She's a smart lady."

Smart enough to know he'd had a rough day and needed some space. She'd been quiet on the ride home, then made herself scarce as soon as they'd reached the cabin. He was lousy company tonight. And she was still upset about Mickey's death.

"When do you want to pick up today's reports?" Gene said, when Brent failed to respond to his comment about Claire.

Even though Brent needed to stay abreast of the team's efforts to locate Forrester, he couldn't face driving back into the city today. Not for the first time, he cursed the cabin's lack of Internet access.

As he tried to summon up the energy to get back in the car, an idea came to him. "How about faxing them to me at the marina near here?"

"The reports are confidential."

"I know the owner. I can be waiting at the fax machine when they come through."

There was a brief pause, then, "I'll have Lisa call when she's ready to send them."

It was a major concession, but Gene didn't give him a chance to thank him. "Read the reports, then get some rest. We've got a lot of work to do tomorrow."

As soon as the call ended, Brent felt his eyelids droop. At first, he was drifting, but then an image flashed in his mind. Sanderson, writhing in a pool of blood while Forrester stood over him, cold-bloodedly counting a wad of cash.

He jerked his eyes open, rubbed hands slick with sweat on the thighs of his jeans.

When Forrester was arrested, he was going to learn that money didn't buy cars in prison.

CLAIRE STUDIED BRENT'S blank face and slumped body. The professionalism he'd used as a shield seemed to have deserted him. He looked worn-out and depressed. She should leave before he noticed her. But over the past few days, her feelings for him had expanded beyond mere physical attraction to include something unexpected.

Friendship.

She must be a glutton for punishment to even

consider talking to him. The last time she'd broached the subject of grief, he'd hit her with that "no trespassers allowed" stare of his and several biting comments. She turned to go, then hesitated as her mother's advice echoed in her head.

A true friend doesn't wait for an invitation to help. A true friend makes the offer and accepts the risk of being told to mind her own business.

With a sigh, she turned back.

"Are you hungry?" she asked.

It took Brent a full twenty seconds to switch his gaze from the lake to her. "No."

"Do you want a drink?"

He grimaced. "No more coffee."

"I wasn't thinking coffee. I was thinking beer or whiskey. If I hunt through the cupboards, will I find some left over from last year?"

"I doubt it."

"We should have stocked up before we left the city."

"Why? So I could get drunk?"

"You've had a rough day," she said, settling into the leather chair opposite him.

"I must be a sorry sight for you to be offering me that." His gaze slid from her face to her breasts and stayed there. "What else are you offering?"

Her breath caught as awareness shot through her. But despite his provocative words, she saw no lust in his eyes. Only despair.

"Not sex," she said quietly. "Friendship."

His gaze backtracked to her face. "Not a good idea to be my friend. Look what happened to Pete."

When she frowned, he waved a hand dismissively. "Forget I said that. I'm just being morbid."

"You can't hang tough all the time."

"Why not?" He shifted restlessly. "Hanging tough sure as hell feels better than hanging by a thread."

"Is that how you feel? Like you're just barely holding on?"

"I can't talk about this," he said in a low voice.

"Yes, you can," she said gently.

She was treading on sensitive ground so it wasn't surprising that he remained silent for a long time.

Finally, he looked at her, his eyes dark with anguish. "Pete died because Forrester's a greedy bastard."

"I know. I'm so sorry."

He shook his head in bewilderment. "I want a rewind button on life. But that's stupid. Pete's gone. End of story."

"It's perfectly natural to feel anger and frustration and grief."

His mouth tightened and his eyes flashed. "You think you know what I'm feeling?"

"Yes, I do."

"Why? Because you've read some psych textbook?"

She had a sense of déjà vu, of coming full circle to where they'd started, and the thought upset her more than she cared to admit. "I thought you were done with cheap shots against my profession."

"That wasn't a cheap shot," he said. "I'm trying to make a point."

"Which is?"

"You can't possibly *know* what I'm feeling because you've never experienced the violent death of someone close to you."

His bitter words stung like a slap in the face. "I understand more about tears and pain than you could ever imagine."

He crossed his arms over his chest, clearly unconvinced.

Should she tell him? She took a deep breath, then plunged ahead. "When I was eighteen, my father put his gun to his right temple and pulled the trigger. His note said it was the only way he could make the nightmares stop. Ten months earlier, he'd been involved in an investigation where innocent bystanders were killed, including a six-year-old girl. He couldn't stop thinking about her and second-guessing his actions. Had he reacted fast enough? Had there been a chance to save her that he'd missed?"

Brent's angry expression was long gone, but a dam had burst inside her and she couldn't stop. "The Bureau sent him to a counselor who was clueless about the complexity of the job, clueless about the kind of split-second decisions agents have to make and live with for the rest of their lives. My father went to a few appointments, then refused to go again. He blamed himself for that death. Six months later, he took his life."

Goose bumps rose on her arms at the memory. "You asked me why I changed my mind about becoming a vet. I did it because of my dad. I promised myself at his graveside that I'd learn enough so that one day I might be able to spare another agent's family the tragedy my mom and I had to endure."

"Claire—"

"Let me finish." She lifted her chin. "With the exception of Mickey, none of the agents I've treated has appreciated my concern and support. And tonight, you've shown me that you're also too closed-minded and cynical for me to help."

She swallowed. "It's hard for me to admit this, but I've been wasting my time. Not anymore. I'm leaving the Bureau."

For a moment, his poker face slipped, and shock took its place. But she didn't feel satisfaction, only sadness that it had taken her so long to see what should have been obvious all along.

She stood up. "Please don't mention my plans to Gene. He has enough on his mind."

"He'll want to know."

"I'll give him sufficient notice." She headed for the hallway, pausing only when she'd reached it. "The day Forrester is in custody, I'm starting a new life far from here."

When Brent awoke the next morning, he had a major hangover—without the enjoyment of having partied hard. Pete's death weighed heavily on him, and he was still reeling from Claire's revelations about her father and her future plans.

Claire had always seemed overly enthusiastic in her desire to help, but now that he knew her underlying motivation, he wished he hadn't given her such a rough time. His foul mood last night was no justification for the scathing remarks he'd made to her. But how could he have known she'd endured her own devastating loss?

It took a lot of courage to counsel others on grief and trauma, especially when doing so must dredge up painful memories of her own. However, Claire seemed to be someone who did what needed to be done, no matter how difficult. There were people who would say the same about him.

Much as he hated to admit it, he owed her an apology.

He took his time, washing, shaving and brushing his teeth. He didn't mind admitting that he was wrong so much as he hated *being* wrong. In a job like his, mistakes could cost lives.

When he could delay no longer, he left the washroom in search of Claire. Her bedroom door was open when he passed by, but she was nowhere in sight. He checked the main room first, then headed into the kitchen. Both places were empty. His heart rate picked up, but he could see his Mustang from the kitchen window so he knew she hadn't snagged his keys and taken off.

Before he could check outside, Claire came through the front door, a turquoise beach towel wrapped like a sarong around her. Obviously, she'd been swimming, and her wet hair dripped onto her exposed left shoulder, leaving the bare skin glistening with moisture. He wondered what kind of bathing suit she was wearing— daring bikini? modest one-piece?—but the oversize towel was excellent camouflage.

Of course, he had no business thinking those thoughts after haranguing her last night.

"How was the water?" he asked.

"Refreshing," was her response.

Well, at least she was speaking to him. Although a one-word answer could hardly be construed as conversation. He decided to see if he could get a full sentence out of her. "Does that mean chilly?"

She gave him a rueful smile. "Yes, but I decided I needed the exercise even if my lips turned blue."

The word "lips" drew his gaze to her mouth like a magnet. Her smile faltered for a moment, and he realized he ran the risk of doing something utterly asinine—like kissing her—if he didn't focus on a different part of her anatomy quickly. He chose her left eyebrow.

"About last night…" He hesitated, unsure whether she'd accept what he had to say.

Her eyebrow rose toward her hairline as she waited for him to continue.

"I know you meant well, and I was being a jerk, but the thing is—"

"You're a very independent person who isn't used to confiding in anyone."

"Am I wrong to want some privacy?"

She took a moment to answer. "I believe it's a lonely way to live. However, that strategy appears to have worked for you."

Had it worked? Or was he just too hard-headed to try another way? Maybe he was ready for a change. The only problem was the person he felt most comfortable talking to was no longer alive. And Claire… Claire was the woman he wanted to share his bed with, not his problems.

She tugged at her towel, which had begun to slip. "I need to get dressed. I don't want to make you late for your meeting with Gene."

He'd assumed some serious groveling would be necessary to clear the air between them, but Claire apparently didn't believe in holding a grudge.

As she turned to go, he touched her arm. "I didn't get a chance to say it last night, but I'm sorry about your father."

"Thanks." She lowered her gaze. "I wanted you to understand why I can empathize about Pete's death, but I was wrong to hit you over the head the way I did."

He grimaced. "That's usually the fastest way to get my attention."

A smile tugged the corner of her mouth. "I'll keep it in mind."

He knew he should quit while he was ahead, but he needed to know something. "Are you really planning to leave the Bureau?"

She tucked a strand of hair behind her ear.

"Yes, I've been offered a position in Minneapolis."

He thought she'd spoken rashly last night, but evidently the idea of resigning had been on her mind.

"I've been undecided," she added. "It took this situation to make me see things clearly."

Unfortunately, the situation she referred to was one involving him. Gene was going to string him up by his thumbs.

"Look, I know I've been…difficult. And last night, I was way out of line—"

"Don't worry. I'll make sure Gene knows my decision has nothing to do with you."

Was he so transparent?

Only to her.

He pushed the unsettling notion away. His concern about Gene's response had been a knee-jerk reaction. What really bothered him was the thought of Claire leaving town. He'd been telling himself that physical attraction was all he felt for her, but he knew now that was a lie. When Forrester was apprehended and the danger was over, he wanted to spend time with her. Watch movies. Go for walks. Make love with her. Show her with his hands and mouth and body the feelings he had so much trouble expressing in words. But none of that could happen if she moved to another state.

"With all the stress of the past few days, are you sure switching careers is the right decision?"

"I won't know if it's a mistake until I do it."

"By then, it may be too late to change things back the way they were."

"I have to take that chance." She captured his gaze, her expression more earnest than he'd ever seen it. "I need to know that my work has a positive impact on my patients' lives. That isn't happening at the Bureau."

He wanted to argue with her, but he didn't know enough about her experience with her FBI patients to be convincing.

Before he could think of anything to say, the ring of his cell phone intruded.

He expected the call to be from Gene, but it was Jim Sharratt.

"The blackmailer called to tell me the location," the older man said, anxiety evident in every word.

"His days of making demands are coming to an end," Brent reassured him.

As he gathered up his notes for the meeting with Gene, he felt the quick thrill of anticipation. Wherever Forrester arranged to pick up his blackmail money, the FBI would be waiting for him.

Chapter Eleven

The trap was set for four o'clock Thursday afternoon, less than two days away.

Claire watched from the sidelines as Gene and Brent worked feverishly to hammer out a plan to capture Forrester. Everything was complicated by the fact that they were after one of their own. They had to jettison their usual deployment and tactical procedures and come up with new ones, something Brent excelled at.

Forrester had instructed Sharratt to leave the money in the office of the Friedberg Book

Manufacturing Company. A call to the company revealed the plant was shut down for the week. Gene wanted to tour the building on Wednesday, but Brent argued Forrester might be watching. They contacted the plant manager at home, who met with them to explain the layout of the building and give the locations of the equipment, shelving units, skids of paper and books in process—anything that might provide cover or a hiding place for the agents needed inside. Once the logistics were sorted out, they held a meeting to brief the dozen agents assigned to the operation.

Claire was to remain with Gene in the surveillance van parked at a neighboring factory. Brent would take cover by the Heidelberg six-color printing press and be the agent closest to the drop-off point.

A new ballistics report indicated that Sanderson had been killed by a weapon previously used in an armed kidnapping by a felon named Hank Totten. The gun had been locked up in evidence storage but was now missing. Forrester had been involved in the initial arrest, making him a likely suspect in the theft. However, the storage facility's records showed that the agent hadn't been on the premises for several months. Brent was convinced that Forrester had visited more recently, so he asked the supervisor to double-check and get back to him.

The only break in preparation came on Wednesday when the team and Claire attended Mickey's funeral. Agents from offices all over the country came to show their respect for Mickey's sacrifice. Claire noticed that even the most stoic among the attendees shed tears during the deeply moving eulogy, which Mickey's best friend gave. The image that stayed with her long after the service ended was of Mickey's fiancée and his mother clinging to each other.

Then it was back to the Bureau to review the plan again.

By late Wednesday night, the last few details of the operation had been finalized. There was nothing left to do but wait.

Claire kept telling herself that every contingency had been anticipated and dealt with, but her nerves were vibrating like a power line in a storm. After a week on the run, Forrester could be so strung out that he'd rather kill than go to prison. And as the agent nearest the blackmail money, Brent would be in the most danger.

"You're going to wear out the carpet," Brent said, glancing up from his laptop.

She stopped in midpace, flopped into a chair. "I wish it was over. Doesn't the waiting get to you?"

"Sometimes." He stretched his arms above his head, settled deeper into the cushions of the couch. "Pete and I used to trade sports trivia to keep from climbing the walls."

"Sports trivia, huh? I wish I knew some."

"I thought psychologists were trained in sophisticated relaxation techniques?"

His voice was slightly mocking, and she finally asked him what she'd wanted to know since they'd met. "What *is* your problem with psychologists?"

His eyes drilled into hers, but she held his stare and didn't look away.

"You really want to know?" he asked.

"Yes, I do."

"You remember asking why I waited so long to join the Bureau?"

She nodded.

He braced his hands on his muscled thighs. "The fact is I applied right after college. Aced every interview. Beat out hundreds of applicants to make it to the final round. Last hurdle was the psych testing…."

Her mouth went dry, but she managed to ask, "It didn't go well?"

"Dr. Telso made it clear that he wouldn't recommend hiring me at the Bureau. *Ever.*"

"Did he explain why?" she murmured.

"He said my temperament was incompatible with being an agent. The word *reckless* came up in the conversation."

That didn't fit with the Brent she knew. He weighed the risks before he took action—even in relationships. But maybe he'd been different back then. "If Dr. Telso was against your being hired, how did it happen?"

"A few years after we met, I was at a convenience store when two thugs armed with shotguns strutted up to the counter and started terrorizing the teenage clerk. If they'd only wanted the money in the till, I wouldn't have intervened. But one of them grabbed the girl by the hair and started dragging her toward the storage room."

Claire felt her stomach drop to her feet. "What happened?"

"I grabbed a can of peaches, nailed the bastard in the head, then tackled the other guy before he could get a shot off."

"That was very brave of you." And dangerous. What if he had missed with that can of fruit?

He shrugged. "Yeah, the local media called me a hero. When I mentioned my dream was to work for the FBI, pressure mounted until Telso caved, and I was allowed into the training program."

"I'm guessing you worked harder than the other recruits to prove you belonged there."

He grinned. "Yeah, I did."

"Are you still trying to prove something? Is that why you nearly went up in flames to rescue Forrester's briefcase?"

His grin disappeared. "You worry too much."

"I'm worried about tomorrow," she admitted.

He leaned forward, his gaze serious. "Tomorrow should run as smoothly as these things ever do."

"I don't like that qualifier," she said, stiffening.

"Complications happen, but the plan's solid. It'll turn out okay."

She knew he was trying to reassure her, but her imagination kept coming up with scenarios in which he was injured or—God forbid—killed. "Why not arrest Forrester as soon as he shows up?"

"And charge him with what? Trespassing?"

Brent crossed his arms over his chest. "We don't have a single witness who can place him at the scene of the crimes he's committed this past week. We need to catch him red-handed with Sharratt's money."

"You think that will be enough to connect him to Sanderson's murder?"

"I think we can make the case that Sanderson could have identified Forrester as Sharratt's blackmailer by what he said to his victim so Forrester killed him to protect a lucrative stream of income. That's a motive the jury can understand and feel good about convicting on."

"How far are you willing to go to make that happen?"

A muscle twitched in his jaw. "Really far. I want to see Forrester in prison."

She couldn't stop herself from saying, "Please be careful."

He nodded, then gave her a sideways glance. "What will you do when we finally lock him up?"

That was easy. "Get on with my life."

"In Minneapolis?"

She tried to read his body language and tone of voice. Did it matter to him if she stayed or went? Would she let his opinion sway her one way or the other? She gave herself a mental shake. She'd already made her decision.

"Yes," she said, then, if only to clarify in her own mind, "in Minneapolis."

His expression gave nothing away, so she asked, "What are the chances that Forrester won't show?"

"He'll show," Brent said firmly. "He wouldn't have contacted Sharratt if he had any inkling we've discovered his blackmail scheme. And he hasn't used his credit cards since he escaped from Ridsdale so he's probably running out of cash."

Cash. The reason he'd murdered Pete Sanderson. The reason he'd threatened Sharratt. Forrester had to be stopped. And no amount of worrying on her part could keep Brent safe.

She had no choice but to trust in tomorrow's plan.

GRIPPING THE SIDES of the printing press's control panel, Brent stretched to restore circulation to his cramped legs. Sharratt had made the drop forty-five minutes ago. Outside, several mobile units were watching for Forrester. When he arrived, Gene would relay the news to the agents waiting inside the plant. In the meantime, Brent concentrated on keeping his muscles limber and his nerves steady.

His thoughts wandered to the previous night's conversation with Claire. He'd never talked to anyone, not even Pete, about his run-in with Telso. The rejection had ripped into him, made him feel weak and stupid and worthless—just like the vicious bullying he'd endured as a kid. He had tried to reason his feelings away, but they had hardened like cement. So he buried them, never anticipating he'd have to deal with a psychologist again.

Then Claire had come into his life.

She was nothing like Telso, but he'd turned his seething animosity for the man on her. She had stood up to him. She had tried to get to know him. She had made repeated attempts to help him.

After everything she'd done, how could he let her walk away?

Screw Minneapolis. She might claim to want a career change, but he knew her decision was motivated by insecurity. And that issue could be dealt with separately from their future.

Could he convince her to stay? Maybe. Did he want her to stay? Definitely. But was it fair to ask her to turn down a job offer when he wasn't sure he wanted—or was even capable of—a long-term relationship?

Claire was the first woman to really interest him since his fiancée had left. He didn't want to miss out on something terrific with her, but he also didn't want to have his heart shredded again.

His earpiece suddenly resonated with Gene's low voice. "Suspect spotted on Elm, driving a light blue Camry sedan, and is headed for the target location. ETA five minutes."

Finally.

Brent murmured into his mouthpiece, confirming that his colleagues inside the plant were in position and ready for action.

The seconds ticked by.

"Everybody, listen up," Gene said. "Emotions

are running high tonight, but if anybody's contemplating a lone-wolf takedown, he risks endangering himself and his fellow agents. This is a team operation, and nothing else will be tolerated."

Gene had directed his remarks to the entire group, but Brent suspected it was a personal warning. If the others hadn't been listening in, he would have told his boss not to worry. He had rehearsed this operation countless times in his mind and believed its success depended on all of them executing their assigned tasks. He had no intention of deviating from the plan to settle a personal score with Forrester.

He felt the tension in the room mount as Gene continued his running commentary.

"Suspect is approaching our location."

Half a minute later, *"Suspect is pulling into the parking lot."*

Then, finally, *"Suspect has left his vehicle."*

Brent withdrew his semiautomatic pistol from his holster and rested it against his jeans-clad thigh. Adrenaline raced through his veins. He forced his breathing to slow, his mind to focus. Soon he'd be face-to-face with the man who had murdered his mentor and best friend, Pete, as well as Harris and Langdon—both agents with promising futures—and who had almost killed Claire and himself.

Forrester's threat to Claire was going to end tonight. He gripped his weapon tightly and waited.

The door on the south end of the building opened, and a funnel of light pierced the darkness. Forrester took his time directing the beam of his flashlight in a wide arc around him. The light moved methodically to each section of the plant. When the beam hit the printing press, Brent's pulse leapt even though he knew he was well concealed and would cast no betraying shadow.

After a few minutes, Forrester seemed satisfied nothing was out of place and redirected the light to his destination: the office. Footsteps—quick and determined—echoed in the cavernous building.

Brent counted the steps until he heard the office door opening. The plan called for him to wait for Forrester to pick up the money and make it halfway back to the exit. At that point, Brent was to spring the trap. Forrester would be caught out in the open, unable to retreat into the office for cover or escape to the exterior.

Brent illuminated the face of his watch and monitored one minute ticking by and then another. What was Forrester doing? he fumed silently. Counting every damn bill?

Finally, the footsteps started again, more quickly this time. Now that Forrester had the money, he was obviously in a hurry to get the hell away.

At the count of twenty-five, Brent spoke into his mouthpiece, "Now."

Ian Alston, who was responsible for rigging the breaker panel, responded by hitting the lights.

Forrester was illuminated in midstride, flashlight in his left hand and Sharratt's canvas bag slung over his shoulder. His right hand immediately went for the gun holstered on his hip.

Stepping in front of the trapped man, Brent aimed his SIG Sauer. "Stop right there, Forrester."

The guy let out a stream of expletives.

Five more agents, all with weapons drawn, fanned out around him.

Like a fish in a net, Brent thought with satisfaction. Forrester's capture was worth every second of planning and waiting.

"You getting this, Gene?" he asked. Alston had set up a camera with the feed going to the surveillance van so Gene and Claire could witness the events playing out inside the plant.

"Oh, yeah."

Brent directed his next words to Forrester. "You know the drill, but I'll say it for the record. This is the FBI, and you are ordered to raise your hands above your head."

Forrester didn't move.

"I said raise your hands, you sonovabitch," Brent said, advancing toward him. "Unless you want to add resisting arrest to the charges of extortion, murder, attempted murder and—"

"What the hell are you talking about?" Forrester interrupted. "All I did was break out of that damn psych hospital, which I should never have been sent to in the first place."

"I'm talking about what you've been doing since you left Ridsdale."

"I've been lying low."

"Arson and bomb-setting are hardly lying low."

"What am I supposed to have set on fire?"

"Your house."

"What?"

Brent hadn't expected a confession, but this I-don't-understand act infuriated him. Did Forrester really think he could con his fellow agents?

"I was there. When the office caught fire, I nearly went up in flames, and Dr. Lamont suffered serious burns to her hand." The memory of those burns—and the blisters they'd turned into a few days ago—made him even angrier.

"Whatever happened had nothing to do with me. I haven't been able to get home for a week."

"Then who knocked out McKenna and put

the bullet in Harris's brain?" he challenged. "Who blew up your rental unit?"

Forrester faltered for a moment, then shot back defiantly, "I have no idea."

"Save it for the jury," Brent said. "Now set your gun down on the floor and kick it toward me. Agent Starr is going to remove any other weapons you're carrying."

Brent saw Forrester glance at the man assigned to search and disarm him, a man he'd worked closely with. Obviously, Starr was thinking the same thing because he said, "I remember when you came to see me and my wife when my baby girl was born. You said I should spend more time at home, raise my daughter right. Now you've left Harris's kids to grow up without their father."

"You can't believe that," Forrester protested.

"Believe you'd turn against one of your own?" Brent interjected, wishing he could continue the interrogation in a locked room with no witnesses. But there was too much at stake to risk the consequences of breaking the rules. "Why not? Harris wasn't even your first victim—Pete Sanderson was."

"I didn't murder him."

"I'm not buying this innocent act."

"You've got it all wrong…." His words trailed off as the exterior door opened.

Brent shot a quick glance in that direction to find Alec McKenna striding into the plant, his gun aimed squarely at Forrester. The agent's arrival was unexpected, as he had been assigned to one of the mobile units tracking Forrester's progress.

"I heard you were having some trouble, and I thought I might be able to help out," McKenna offered by way of explanation. Then, to Forrester he said, "There's no way out, Andy. It's over."

Forrester's gaze darted from McKenna to Brent to the other armed men surrounding him. Brent had seen the same expression of fear and panic in the eyes of other criminals he'd arrested. Fight or flight usually followed.

"Don't do anything stupid, Forrester."

Forrester shook his head. "There's so much you don't know."

A sense of unease skittered along Brent's nerve endings. "We'll talk about it later."

If Forrester heard him, he didn't give any indication. Instead, the man ran straight at him.

Shots rang out. Somebody shouted a warning.

Too late.

A bullet slammed into Brent's chest.

As he fell to the ground, there was only one thought in his mind: Getting shot wasn't part of the plan.

Chapter Twelve

Claire cried out as she watched Brent go down. Her gaze had been avidly fixed on the closed-circuit monitor in the van throughout the operation, and while she'd sensed the mounting tension in the factory, she hadn't been prepared for Forrester's decision to bolt or the terror that struck her heart when Brent was shot.

Everything had happened so fast. She wasn't even sure who had pulled the trigger or how many bullets had been fired in the warehouse. The only thing that mattered to her was that Brent had been hit.

Her stomach churned and bile burned her throat, but she couldn't tear her gaze away from the horrifying image on the monitor. Brent lay on the factory's concrete floor, possibly dying, and she was trapped in this van, too far away to do anything. She couldn't hold him in her arms or look into his eyes or tell him she loved him.

Her heart skipped a beat. Oh, no. No way could she have fallen in love with Brent. She knew better. At least the logical part of her did.

No, she wasn't in love with him. She was just shaken up by what she'd seen, and yes, worried about him. He'd saved her life twice. Now he could be dying, his blood—

Her heart skipped another beat as she squinted at the monitor. In the back of her mind she was sure she hadn't seen any blood, but the other agents were crowded around Brent, obscuring her view.

"Claire."

She felt a hand on her shoulder, making her start.

"Brent's going to be fine," Gene said, searching her eyes.

"How do you know? He's not moving."

"He's wearing a Kevlar vest under his jacket."

"What?" The words took a moment to penetrate her fear.

"It's standard gear in this kind of operation."

"But he went down so hard—"

"The force of the bullet."

Gene's gaze shifted away from hers, and his next words indicated he was listening to a report over his earpiece. "Ian says Brent's going to have a beauty of a bruise, that's all."

She didn't know whether to laugh or cry. "You're sure he's all right?"

Gene nodded. "I took a bullet that way about two years ago, and while it's not fun, it sure as hell beats the alternative."

"No kidding," she said wryly.

She glanced back at the monitor in time to see one of the other agents help Brent to his feet. He turned to look at something behind him.

At first, she saw only a pool of dark liquid. Blood, she realized, and felt her stomach churning again. It was apparent from the size of the pool that someone had taken a bullet somewhere the vest didn't protect. Either that, or someone had failed to wear one at all.

When Brent moved aside, she saw that it was Forrester who lay motionless on the concrete floor.

And she knew from his open, unseeing eyes that he would never threaten her—or anybody else—again.

BRENT HAD IMAGINED dozens of scenarios in which Forrester was captured, but he'd always expected the bastard to go to prison, not wind up dead. Not that he was sorry. Forrester was a cold-blooded murderer who had ended the lives of men better than himself. If he hadn't died, he would have retained a clever lawyer and challenged every piece of evidence against him. Now that wouldn't happen. Now there was no chance Forrester would get away with his crimes.

So why wasn't he satisfied with tonight's outcome?

He glanced at Claire, who was driving the Mustang, then back at the winding road. A recent rain had washed away most of the gravel, making the last few miles of the ride uncomfortably bumpy. The jarring motion aggravated the bruise on his chest, and he was glad there wasn't much farther to go.

It was almost midnight when he and Claire reached the cabin, but neither of them was in any mood to sleep. They settled themselves on the couch in the living room.

"Forrester was completely surrounded," Claire said suddenly. "Why would he think he could escape?"

Brent had been wondering the same thing. Because as much as he couldn't regret Forrester's death, he didn't fully understand the circumstances surrounding it. "Maybe he just flipped out. I've seen it go down that way before. A guy suddenly realizes it's the end of the line for him, and he can't cope."

She shivered. "And you got caught in the crossfire."

"It happens." That didn't mean he hadn't felt a moment of stark terror when the bullets started flying and he was hit.

"I didn't even see who fired," she admitted.

"McKenna and Metzger both did."

"Who hit you?"

"McKenna claimed it was him, but he could be covering for Metzger, who's only been with the Bureau for a short time. Their guns have been collected, and Ballistics will determine the owner of the bullet that hit me and the ones that killed Forrester."

During the mandatory investigation that followed the discharge of an agent's weapon, both McKenna and Metzger would be called upon to defend their decisions to use deadly force.

"If Forrester had given up his weapon when I first ordered him to," Brent said, "he'd still be alive tonight."

"He must have known it was dangerous to hang on to it."

"Maybe it's a case of 'suicide by cop.'"

"You think he wanted to die? Why?"

"I'm guessing he couldn't stand the thought of going to prison."

If he was right, Forrester had executed one last selfish act before his death. Agents who killed in the line of duty often suffered from guilt. McKenna was a seasoned agent with years of experience, but Metzger wasn't. How would Metzger cope, especially if the investigation concluded that Forrester had meant no harm to anyone but himself?

Brent immediately thought of Claire. Her job was to support agents through such difficult times. That's what she'd been trying to do with him. Yet he'd rejected her every effort.

That was going to change, starting now.

"Tonight didn't turn out the way I expected at all," he said, "and not just because I was shot and Forrester died. I thought apprehending Pete's killer would make me feel triumphant or at least satisfied that he hadn't gotten away with murder."

"How do you feel?"

He scrubbed at an ink spot on his jeans. "Disappointed, cheated somehow." He glanced over at her. "Does that make sense?"

She nodded. "For the past week, you've been concentrating so hard on capturing Forrester that I think you may have lost sight of something."

At his quizzical look, she smiled sadly. "Punishing him won't bring back Pete."

He felt his throat burn. She was right. Vengeance wasn't as sweet as people said. The pain didn't magically disappear or even lessen. But talking relieved some of the pressure.

"The day I met Pete was the luckiest one of my life. Not just because he had my back when I was new and inexperienced, but because he came to be my best friend."

"It's wonderful you two had such a close relationship."

"Some days we'd shoot hoops at his house, whooping and hollering like lunatics. Other days we'd fish in the lake, enjoying the silence and solitude." He struggled for control for a long moment, before continuing in an unsteady voice. "He was more than my best friend. He was the father I never had."

"I'm so sorry, Brent." She shifted closer and lay a comforting hand on his shoulder.

"I'm not sure I can accept him being gone yet." He closed his eyes, rested his head on the back of the couch.

"There's no timetable for grief," she said. "You can't rush it, you just have to deal with it when you're ready."

Her words sounded wise, but right now he was content just listening to her voice. It reminded him of a summer breeze, soft and relaxing. He felt himself unwind for the first time since the beginning of the stakeout for Forrester.

"It took me six months to accept my dad was lost to me," she said unexpectedly. "I kept telling myself he was on assignment and would show up in the kitchen and ask me to bake tiger brownies for him."

Brent opened his eyes and waited, hoping she would continue.

After a moment, she did. "I couldn't deal with the way he'd died. And I was angry and upset about the note he left for me." She stopped, bit her lip.

Brent looped his arm over her and drew her against his side. "Tell me about it," he murmured.

"I've never told anyone," she admitted softly. "Not even my mom."

He remained silent, letting her decide.

She inhaled deeply, then expelled the breath in a sigh. "He wrote that every time he looked at me, he remembered that little girl—the one who had died during the airline hostage rescue. Her family had been deprived of seeing her grow up, attend college, get married. And although he loved me and wanted the best for me, it was impossible for him to watch me enjoy those experiences." Her lips trembled, but she kept on doggedly. "He took his life because he couldn't stop obsessing about somebody else's daughter."

Brent held her closer, incredulous that a father could be so lost in despair, he wouldn't realize the agony his suicide would inflict on his child.

"He needed help," she said, "and he didn't get it. I couldn't let the same thing happen to another agent, another family."

Brent brushed her hair back from her eyes. "He'd be proud of you, Claire."

"I like to think so."

"How could he not be?" he said quietly. "You're sensitive and caring. You try to help people. You've helped *me* despite my making it difficult for you."

If someone had told him ten days ago that he would be having this conversation with a woman—especially one who was a psychologist—he'd have scoffed. But a lot had happened in the interval, and the best part was Claire.

"Your patients are lucky to have your special insight."

She looked away and traced the edge of the couch with her fingertips. "You really think that I can make a difference?"

"I know it."

The tentative smile that curved her lips gave him hope that she might stay.

CLAIRE HUGGED her arms to her body.

Brent had finally let down his barriers. He had shared his grief and loneliness over Pete's death with her. And his openness had, in turn, made it possible for her to reveal things about her father's suicide that she'd never told anyone before. She felt purged, released, and closer to Brent than she'd ever imagined.

She didn't realize she was crying until he reached over and brushed a tear from her cheek. It was a gentle, fleeting touch. Yet somehow the brief contact charged the space between them. She met his gaze. His eyes reflected the same desire that she felt. For days, she'd been telling herself that physical intimacy with Brent would be a mistake because they weren't emotionally close. But their relationship had undergone a transformation. Honesty had forged a unique rapport, drawing them together, leading them relentlessly to this moment when the attraction between them needn't be denied any longer.

Having already shared pain, they deserved to share pleasure, too. And she couldn't imagine a pleasure more intense, more joyful, than making love with Brent. This time, there would be no denying impulses, no stopping in the midst of passion.

With hungry eagerness, she pressed her lips to his throat...his jaw...his mouth....

BRENT DREW AN UNSTEADY breath, confused—and aroused—by the blatant sexuality in Claire's kisses. He was hanging on to control by a rapidly fraying rope. "This isn't a good idea."

"Sure, it is." She ran her hands up his shirt front, immediately pulling away when he sucked in a sharp breath. "What's wrong?"

He'd wanted her hands on him for so long. Now that she apparently wanted the same thing, he was frustrated that her touch had made him flinch. "I'm just a little sore where the bullet hit," he told her.

"I was terrified when I saw you fall," she admitted, as she unfastened the buttons on his shirt.

Pushing the fabric aside, she gasped at the starburst of red and blue and purple that marked his skin. He wondered if she was repulsed by the sight of his bruise, but then she tipped her head and kissed his chest.

Her lips whispered gently over the tender skin, tracing the outline of the bruise.

"What—" He swallowed as her mouth

cruised lightly over his nipple. "What are you doing?"

"Kissing it better." She glanced up at him, a smile teasing the corners of her mouth. "Is it working?"

"Yeah. I…think it is."

Her smile widened. "Good."

Her mouth moved against his skin, tracing his collarbone, skimming up his neck until her lips brushed against his.

"Nothing's changed since last time we kissed," he said thickly.

She pushed his shirt over his shoulders. "You don't really believe that, do you?"

No. No, he didn't. He had bared his soul to Claire tonight and had no regrets about it. His only regret was that she had plans to leave town.

But maybe those plans weren't definite. Maybe she was still mulling over her options.

Why else would she be willing to make love with him? She wasn't a one-night-stand kind of woman. Her actions suggested that she, too, wanted to give their relationship a chance.

Then again, coherent thought was next to impossible when she was touching him.

She smiled as if she understood. "One thing that's changed is my mind."

"Woman's prerogative?"

She tossed her blond head. "Don't look a gift horse in the mouth."

He studied her. "You are a gift. A beautiful, sexy gift—"

"—who's waiting to be unwrapped," she finished boldly.

His mouth turned dry as chalk. "Are you sure?"

It was his last attempt to resist her—although he could no longer remember why he had ever believed he should.

"I'm absolutely sure." She stroked her finger-tips down his arm. "Unless your injury—"

"What injury?"

She gave him another dazzling smile, a wordless reassurance that she wanted him as much as he wanted her.

He kissed her, deep ravenous kisses that left them both panting for more. Their tongues collided. Their teeth nipped at each other. Their tastes mingled to become one.

Eventually, with her eyes encouraging him, he reached for the hem of her blouse. He eased it over her head, then undid her bra and freed her lovely breasts. Her nipples were just as sensitive as he remembered. They hardened immediately, stimulated by his admiring gaze. He bent his head so he could suckle her, his tongue swirling over one peak, then the other.

She gasped, her blond hair tickling his wrists. He pressed his lips under her left breast, where he could feel her heart beating fast. He wanted to drive her wild. Make her burn for him. As he burned for her.

He shifted position until she was lying on top of him. As he threaded his fingers through her luxurious, thick hair, he marveled at how beautiful, how desirable she was. How had he ever managed not to touch her?

The mating of their mouths made him hunger for a more intimate coupling, but he wasn't about to rush her. She would let him know when she was ready.

After a moment, she eased into a kneeling position astride him. Bracing her hands on his biceps, she moved her pelvis provocatively against him. He felt himself grow harder. He was tempted to crush her to him, but he resisted to savor every delicious sensation. He traced the features of her lovely, flushed face. She parted her lips and sighed his name. He caressed her neck, her shoulders, her beautiful breasts. She slipped her hand under the waistband of his jeans.

He caught his breath. Felt her touch him through the cotton of his BVDs. Anticipation was an exquisite torment—one he wasn't sure he could endure for very long. He breathed in the fragrance of her skin, her hair. She was an erotic dream come true. Her soft, sweet mouth made him ache. Her seeking hand drove him mad. He couldn't remember ever wanting a woman so desperately. When her fingers closed over him, he felt as if he were going to explode.

Gritting his teeth, he fought for control. No good. He'd yearned for her too long. With a groan, he pulled her to him and rolled until they lay on their sides.

"Hey," she said.

"Protection," he panted, reaching for his wallet.

She tugged down his zipper. "Looking out for me yet again," she murmured.

He kicked off his jeans and underwear, while she did the same, then he quickly covered himself with the condom. He rolled back on top of her, exhaling deeply as their legs tangled together. Damn, she felt good. So good. So right.

She urged him closer. Her mouth nibbled a wet path along his shoulder, her fingers gripped his back fiercely as she whispered passionate entreaties against his skin. "Please…I can't… wait…anymore."

"Look at me," he murmured.

She opened her eyes. They were dark with desire, clouded with passion.

"I want to see you," he said. "And I want to know you see me."

She smiled. "I want you inside me."

It was what he wanted, too, more than anything. He entered her slowly, prolonging the moment, heightening the pleasure for both of them. Then he began to move, responding to her excited breathing and caresses.

She twisted under him as he alternated shallow, controlled thrusts with deeper, wilder ones. She squeezed his buttocks and rubbed her breasts wantonly against his chest. Her uninhibited responses quickly shattered his rhythm—and his willpower. He didn't want this union to end, but the need for release became overwhelming.

She seemed to share his sense of urgency. "Now," she gasped, lifting her hips off the couch.

"Now," he breathed, plunging into her fully.

Her body went rigid. A heartbeat later,

tremors convulsed her, and her inner muscles contracted around him. She expelled her breath in a deep, satisfied moan. The sound resonated inside him, and his control snapped. As his climax hit hard and fast, a shout escaped him. Then he collapsed on top of her.

"I wouldn't have guessed you were a screamer," she said a moment later, but her voice held no censure, just a purring contentment.

"I'm not," he mumbled.

"So what happened?" She rubbed her toes along his leg.

He cracked open one eye. "You."

"I'll take that as a compliment."

"It was intended as one."

She pressed her lips to his shoulder. He didn't want her to let him go. Not now. Not in an hour. Not anytime in the foreseeable future. His heart skipped a beat at the disconcerting thought. It wasn't his way to think long term. Life was too uncertain. Situations tended to be fluid, and he had learned to go with the flow.

But Claire wasn't comfortable with uncertainty. She liked to know what to expect next, liked to make plans. She had made a plan to leave the Bureau.

Tonight had proved their relationship deserved more time. Claire was the first woman he'd felt sexually *and* emotionally compatible with, and he wasn't about to be cheated out of her company because she was having second thoughts about her career.

Tomorrow, he'd convince her to make a new plan that included him.

Chapter Thirteen

Whistling under his breath, Brent dug through the kitchen cupboards for coffee supplies. This morning he didn't need caffeine to clear his foggy brain. Claire had done that with a few suggestive words and some bare skin. He definitely liked her way of waking up better.

He found the filters, and soon the smell of freshly brewed coffee filled the kitchen. As he poured the hot, dark liquid into two stoneware mugs, he heard footsteps. He glanced over his shoulder.

Claire wore black shorts and a bright red

T-shirt. He let his gaze skim over her, from her bare toes, up the length of her shapely legs, to slim hips, a slender waist, perfect breasts and graceful shoulders. Her skin glowed, and her lips looked slightly swollen from his kisses. She made appreciative noises about the coffee, but he noticed her gaze slid away from his quickly.

Uh-oh. Regrets?

Her reaction stung more than he wanted to admit. Their lovemaking shouldn't be something she regretted. She had been the one to come on to him last night, not the other way around. And again this morning.

Turning to face her, he planted his butt against the counter and folded his arms across his chest. *What was her problem?*

She glanced at Forrester's CD on the kitchen table.

His anger vanished in sudden under-standing.

With him next to her, she'd been able to forget what had brought them together. But left alone, she'd remembered the threat to her was gone, and Brent was no longer responsible to protect her. There was no reason for them to stay at the cabin any longer. No reason for them not to go their separate ways. No reason unless they wanted to be together.

Closing the distance between them, he pulled her into his arms.

AFTER A MOMENT's hesitation, Claire relaxed against the solid wall of Brent's chest. Her worries had been for nothing. Brent showed no signs of wanting to cut and run.

She eased back from him. "How about I make pancakes to go with that coffee?"

He stroked her hair with his fingertips. "I

wish I could stay, but a debriefing meeting is scheduled at ten."

"Call me when you're free." She remembered her mother saying the exact same words to her father more times than she could count. Of course, this situation was different. Brent didn't owe her an update on his activities—or anything else.

He frowned. "Before I go, there's something I want us to talk about."

An uncomfortable suspicion niggled at her. Was he concerned that she'd have unrealistic expectations about the two of them because of their lovemaking? *Did* she have unrealistic expectations?

"What is it?" she asked.

He hesitated, and her uneasiness grew.

"I don't want you to leave the Bureau," he finally said.

Definitely not what she'd been expecting.

He must have seen her confusion because he blew out a frustrated breath. "I think we're good together. I want to see more of you. But if you take that job in Minneapolis, this will be over before it really gets under way."

Happiness welled up inside her because he wanted to keep seeing her, but she held it in check. What kind of relationship did he have in mind? Casual? Or serious? It was too soon to know if they could be soul mates, but she didn't want to get in any deeper if his attitude toward commitment hadn't changed.

"You want us to date?" she asked cautiously.

He nodded.

Disappointment butted up against the blossoming hope. "Does our dating stand a chance of becoming anything more?"

He eyed her warily. "What do you mean?"

"You told me you didn't believe that people

in your line of work should get married or have kids."

His whole body stiffened. "I know we've come a long way in a short time, but don't you think discussing marriage is kind of premature?"

"Of course it is."

He relaxed noticeably.

"You're asking me to turn down a terrific career opportunity, and I'm not willing to do that for a date or two."

"Claire—"

"What if I stay here and fall in love with you? What then?" She wasn't about to admit to him that it had already happened.

He shifted uncomfortably. "I don't think we can predict the future."

"I know that," she said, her voice rising in exasperation. "I'm not asking for guarantees.

Just some reassurance that your heart isn't completely closed."

His eyebrows slammed together. "I'm surprised you didn't ask me this before we got naked last night."

Now she was the one who felt uncomfortable. "I don't regret making love, if that's what you mean. Being with you was an incredible, unforgettable experience." She smiled even though part of her felt like crying. "But I want to know if there are limits on our relationship. Is that so unreasonable?"

He shook his head. "You deserve to have what you want."

Could he be the man to give it to her? She didn't dare ask him. Instead, she said, "What do *you* want?"

He hesitated. "I thought I knew, but now... I'm not sure."

He could have told her what she wanted to

hear, but he was too honest to take the easy way out. It was one of the things she admired about him, but the hurt made it difficult to continue the conversation.

"You're going to be late," she murmured.

"Do you want to come with me?"

She shook her head. At this point, they could use the time apart to sort through their feelings.

"I'll be back as soon as I can," he said.

"I'll be here."

He started toward her, as if he intended to kiss her good-bye, but she turned away. As much as she'd enjoyed his embrace earlier, she was feeling too raw and vulnerable to let him touch her now.

"This isn't finished," he said from the doorway.

He was right. Nothing had been resolved. Even so, she felt a sense of relief that their conversation would be postponed until later. Hopefully, she'd know what to do then.

AN HOUR LATER, Claire stood gazing out at the lake. The sun had disappeared behind the clouds, but its absence didn't detract from the beauty of the place or the peace she had come to know here. She was going to miss this view. But much more than that, she was going to miss Brent.

She'd reached a conclusion, one that was hard to accept, yet ultimately realistic. Despite everything that had happened between them, they weren't destined to be a couple. No amount of discussion was going to alter his attitude toward commitment. If he promised her anything more now, it would only be because she'd pressured him into it. Her heart would end up broken when he realized a long-term relationship wasn't what he truly wanted.

Having made a decision about Brent, she now needed to do the same about her career. If she remained at the Bureau, Brent's presence would be a constant reminder of what she wanted but couldn't have. Only a masochist would subject herself to that kind of pain, especially when there was a ready alternative. She would take the job at Balanced Life Consulting Group and move to Minneapolis. Once there, she'd be so busy adjusting to her new environment, she'd have little time to brood about Brent.

She was tempted to call Marcy Dearborne, CEO of the company, knowing if she made that commitment, she wouldn't back out of it. But she felt she owed Gene the courtesy of quitting her job with him before accepting another.

She punched in his number, then chewed on her fingernail as she waited for the call to connect.

When Gene came on the line, she cleared her throat. "It's Claire. Do you have a minute?"

"Yeah, I'm between meetings."

She knew this wasn't the ideal time to break her news, but she wanted it over with. "I've decided to resign from my position at the Bureau."

"What the hell are you talking about?"

She cringed at the harshness of his tone. "I've given it a lot of thought, and I don't think the Bureau's the right place for me anymore."

"Why not?" Gene demanded.

Because Brent works there. She couldn't say that, and it wasn't the whole story, anyway. She'd been dissatisfied for months. "I don't feel that I'm helping anybody."

"You know these guys, Claire. They don't wear their hearts on their sleeves, but they still have problems. You're great at getting people to open up to you."

"Maybe in the past," she conceded. "But right now, I'm burned out."

There was a pause at the other end of the line. "This is Brent's doing, isn't it?"

"I was thinking about quitting before I ever met Brent."

"Why don't you come in tomorrow so we can talk—"

"There's no point," she interrupted. "I've made up my mind."

Silence stretched between them.

When Gene finally spoke, the bewilderment in his voice was nearly palpable. "Are you sure you're leaving for the right reason?"

She should be able to answer his question without hesitation, but the words wouldn't come. Her thoughts about Brent and the Bureau had become hopelessly intertwined, and she couldn't seem to separate one from the other. Would she look back one day and realize she'd left a job she was uniquely qualified to do simply because of a failed romance? Or was she only second-guessing what she knew in her heart to be the right decision because of her feelings for Brent?

"I...I have to go now," she said, her voice hoarse with suppressed emotion. "I'll call you later to finalize the details."

Intending to be on her way soon, she packed her carry case and set it by the front door. It was hard to believe only a week had passed since she'd caught her first glimpse of the cabin. In that short time, she'd grown surprisingly attached to the place, but it was an attachment she knew she had to let go of. Just as she knew she had to let go of Brent.

It wasn't easy. She still felt a lingering hope that somehow she and Brent could resolve their differences and become a couple who laughed and loved and shared life together. But she knew better. She would never marry Brent. She would never raise a family with him. Part of her rebelled against such defeatist thinking. Other people managed to turn their dreams into reality. Why couldn't she?

Brent had the capacity to love deeply. His feelings for Pete proved that. Was she naive to think he would one day fall as irrevocably in love with her as she had with him? What if he never realized their relationship was worth committing to? She'd have squandered a great job opportunity. At least her new job wouldn't require patient assessments, so she couldn't mess up as she had with Forrester. Misreading him was the biggest mistake she'd ever made. For her own peace of mind, she needed to figure out where she'd gone wrong. Only then would she be able to move on.

She thought back to her sessions with him, and to last night at the manufacturing plant when she'd watched him on the monitor. What was she missing? Why did she believe him guilty of blackmail, but not the other crimes? Was it professional pride obscuring her perception? A reluctance to accept that Brent had been right and she had been wrong?

No. It was Forrester's shocked expression when accused of attempted murder, arson and bomb-setting. But his denials had been cut short by McKenna's arrival on the scene. She remembered Gene cursing beside her in the van. Despite specific orders to his team, one member had flown solo. After that, chaos had reigned.

She'd been terrified for Brent at the time, but now she was able to consider the events objectively.

Why *had* the plan gone to hell? Because Forrester had panicked.

What had set him off? Brent believed he'd

been overwhelmed by the prospect of prison, but there could be another explanation. Maybe Forrester had realized he'd been set up to take the fall for crimes committed since his escape from Ridsdale and that the person responsible wouldn't let him stay alive to defend himself.

Who had worked other operations with Forrester? Who had survived the attack at his house with only a bloodied scalp? Who had left his surveillance position to come to the plant, then taunted Forrester with the words, "It's over," before firing his weapon?

McKenna.

No wonder she'd experienced uneasiness when she had met him. Her subconscious had been warning her to beware.

She considered calling Gene again, but her suspicions concerning McKenna would likely be met with the same skepticism as her doubts about Forrester. For the FBI to launch an investigation into one of their own, she needed proof.

How could she possibly come up with that proof?

No physical evidence or eyewitness had been found for any of the crimes committed after Forrester's escape from Ridsdale—

The escape from Ridsdale.

McKenna couldn't have engineered that alone. Someone inside Ridsdale must have been involved. And her internal radar had already zeroed in on the staff member responsible.

She called the facility and requested that Maria Gomez pick up a personal call in the office on the second floor, away from her regular workstation.

A few minutes later, the nurse came on the line. "Hello?"

"My name is Dr. Lamont. I'm the psychologist who was with Brent Young, the FBI agent you spoke with a few days ago."

"How can I help you?" Maria asked coolly.

"First, I want to assure you that I'm calling on a disposable cell phone so there's no way anyone can listen in. Second, you should know that Andy Forrester is dead."

"What?" The coolness was gone from her voice.

"Your former patient, the one you helped to escape, was shot and killed last night."

"You heard me tell that agent I had nothing to do with him getting out." There was desperation and anxiety in her voice, confirming for Claire that her initial suspicions had been correct.

"I think you said that because you were scared. Scared of the man who pressured you into getting involved in the first place. You now have a chance to stop being scared and fight back."

The nurse took a moment to respond. "Why should I listen to you?"

"Because you can get this man locked up. All you have to do is identify him for the FBI and tell them that he threatened you."

"He did worse than that," Maria said, her voice trembling with emotion. "He threatened my children."

"Tell me about it," Claire murmured.

"The day after Forrester was admitted to the hospital, a stranger stopped me in the parking lot. He knew a lot about my kids—their ages, their babysitter's name and address. Then he told me if I wanted to keep them safe, I'd better think of a way to get Forrester out."

Claire closed her eyes, imagining the young mother's terror.

"Those kids are my life," Maria whispered.

"I couldn't risk something happening to them that I had the power to prevent."

"I understand," Claire assured her. She didn't know of any parents who could withstand that kind of pressure.

The other woman let out a sigh. "When I heard how many people Forrester had hurt since his escape, I had second thoughts about what I'd done. But it was too late by then, and I was still so afraid for my family."

"I don't believe Forrester was responsible for any of that. I think he was framed by the same man who threatened you."

"Do you know who that man is?"

Claire hesitated. If she revealed McKenna's name, Maria's positive identification of him might later be challenged in the courts. But the media had been all over the plant within minutes of the shooting. If McKenna was visible in their footage of the event and Maria picked him out on her own, there wouldn't be a problem.

"Are you near a TV?" she asked the nurse.

"There's one across the hall in the lunch-room."

"Turn on a news channel. See if there's any coverage of Forrester's shooting."

A few minutes later, Maria Gomez returned. "He was there, the man who threatened my children. His name is Alec McKenna and he's an FBI agent." She sounded shocked by this realization, and even more terrified.

"FBI or not, he will pay for what he's done if you're willing to come forward and tell your story." A long silence followed her words.

"I'll do it," the nurse responded finally. "I want him locked up. That way, I'll know my children are safe."

Claire agreed wholeheartedly with her reasoning. "You need to talk to his supervisor,

Gene Welland, at the Bureau. Call him immediately, tell him who you are and everything
that you just told me."

THE DE-BRIEFING seemed to last forever.
McKenna, Metzger, Alston and Howard recalled hearing a warning shout before the
first shot was fired, Brent, Starr and Cobb remembered hearing it afterward, and the rest
thought the two had happened simultaneously.
Fortunately, the recording from the van was
available to settle the matter. McKenna had
shouted a warning a split second *after* he'd
opened fire.

Brent was grateful when Gene called a short
break to deal with an operational issue.

Twenty minutes later, they reconvened in
the meeting room.

"We're missing someone," Gene said, looking around the table.

"McKenna," Metzger supplied.

Brent glanced through the open doorway in time to see McKenna being hailed by Lisa Conrad, Gene's administrative assistant. The agent made a quick detour to her desk, where she passed him a slip of paper.

Brent saw him look down at the note as he headed toward the meeting room. His steps faltered, and his mouth tightened into a thin line. Whatever he'd seen had obviously displeased him, but he made no mention of it when he rejoined the group.

"Okay, let's see if we can reach a consensus," Gene said.

When Brent glanced around the table, he noticed McKenna staring at him intently. Something in the other man's expression made the hair rise on the back of his neck. Then McKenna looked away, and Brent figured the man simply had a lot on his mind.

Several minutes later, McKenna clutched his stomach. "I think the pizza I ate last night was rotten. My gut's been killing me all morning."

Excusing himself, he headed for the door. "If I don't make it back, you know I went home to puke in my own toilet."

"More information than we really needed to know," Metzger said, rolling his eyes.

Brent doubted McKenna's exit had anything to do with food poisoning. More likely the agent was sick and tired of the whole debriefing process and wanted to skip out. As Gene launched into more discussion of the prior night's events, Brent wished he could escape, too.

Finally, Gene ended with, "I want reports from everybody on my desk tomorrow."

Tomorrow worked for him, Brent thought. He had things to do today—like picking up flowers for Claire and making dinner reservations for them at Gencarelli's, his favorite Italian restaurant. After a terrific meal and a few glasses of red wine, he'd explain that he'd never felt more optimistic about a relationship, and he couldn't see it ending anytime soon. Hopefully, Claire would see that as a positive sign and put the brakes on her moving plans.

Gene's next words nixed his plans. "I'd like you to hang back after the meeting's over, Brent. There's something we need to discuss."

ALEC MCKENNA strode angrily through the Bureau's parking lot.

He should be feeling good today. Forrester was dead, killed before he could implicate him in either the blackmail scheme or Sanderson's murder. Not his original plan, which had called for Forrester to be blown up when he visited his beloved Trans Am at the storage unit. Instead, Langdon had triggered the bomb and Young had found Forrester's backup copy of their blackmail files.

In hindsight, he should never have arranged Forrester's escape from Ridsdale. But he didn't know what Forrester might let slip if they used drugs on him. And he no longer trusted a partner whose conversations with the Bureau psychologist had led to his being locked up.

With Forrester at large, he became the prime suspect for the attacks on Claire Lamont and he would have been blamed if she had been killed. Now that he was dead, the psychologist would have been safe—if the nurse at Ridsdale had stayed scared and silent.

When he reached his car, he reread Maria Gomez's message that Lisa had asked him to deliver to Gene. "Claire Lamont recommended that I contact you about an urgent matter." The nurse probably thought that mentioning the name of the Bureau's psychologist would lend more credibility to her request.

His risk of exposure had never been greater.

Two women were to blame for that.

Neither of them would live to see another dawn.

Chapter Fourteen

"What did you want to talk to me about?" Brent asked, as he followed Gene into his office. Although he could hardly refuse his supervisor's request for a private meeting, he was anxious to get back to the cabin—and Claire.

"Close the door," Gene said.

"This sounds serious."

"Claire's given me her resignation."

Brent frowned as he lowered himself into a chair. Claire had said she was in no hurry to tell Gene she was quitting.

"When did you talk to her?" he asked.

"She called me this morning before you arrived."

Brent's mouth went dry. He'd thought he and Claire were in the negotiating phase. How could she have acted without talking to him?

Gene was watching him, so he added quietly, "Maybe she'll change her mind."

"I don't think so. When I spoke to her, she was adamant about leaving. I probably shouldn't be discussing this with you, but I've known Claire a long time, and this has come as a big shock to me. If you have any ideas about how to convince her to stay, I'd like to hear them."

He resisted the urge to squirm in his chair. "Did she say why she's quitting?"

"She said she didn't think her counseling was doing the men any good." Gene leaned his elbows on the table, made a steeple of his fingers and regarded Brent over them. "I'm not convinced that's the real reason."

"She's mentioned her doubts to me, too."

"Then she's wrong, plain and simple," Gene said. "Anybody who has ever dealt with her professionally has benefited a lot."

Brent wasn't surprised. How many times had he rebuffed her? And yet she'd continued to offer him her empathy and support.

"In fact," Gene continued, "that's one of the reasons I suggested you use your cabin as a safe house for her."

Brent felt as if he'd been sucker-punched. "You're saying you set me up?"

"In the best possible way," his boss assured him. "I knew you were tangled up about Pete's death but too stubborn to go for counseling. And Claire needed protection from Forrester. I figured that if I threw you alone together in a secluded place, you'd both get what you needed."

Brent didn't know about Claire, but he had certainly gotten more than he needed. Making love with her and waking up beside her had been two of the sweetest experiences of his adult life. He wanted to share intense conversations and comfortable silences with her. He wanted to come home to her at the end of the day.

The thought pulled him up short, but he had no time to dwell on it because Gene had started speaking again.

"I can't tell you how disappointed I am that she's leaving. She's been a valuable resource to the agents in this office."

"She doesn't believe that," Brent reminded him.

"She's wrong. Last year, our departmental budget was tight, and the finance guys really pushed hard for me to cut in-house counseling."

"They wanted you to fire Claire?" He couldn't help but feel indignant on her behalf.

"I was dead set against making the cut," Gene said, "but I knew I'd have to defend my position so I e-mailed every agent I'd sent her way. I asked them for their input, whether they'd found talking to her helpful or not. Their response was overwhelmingly positive."

"Did you keep those e-mails?" Brent asked.

"As a matter of fact, I did." Gene rummaged through the bottom drawer of his credenza, found what he was searching for and pulled out a thick envelope. "I had planned to show them to her at her next performance review, but it doesn't look like I'll get that chance."

"She needs to know she's made a difference."

"I agree." He passed the sealed envelope

across the desk. "I don't know that this will change her mind about leaving, but I don't want Claire doubting the impact of the work she did here."

Brent nodded. "I'll be sure to give this to her."

"You can also tell her that I'm grateful— not just for what she did for those agents, but for what she did for me. Without Claire, it's unlikely I'd be celebrating my anniversary tomorrow."

Gene's admission was surprising because the supervisor rarely mentioned his personal life. Brent rose to his feet, anxious to take the file to Claire.

"I still think there's more to her decision to leave than job dissatisfaction," Gene said. "And if it has anything to do with her relationship with you, I want you to think long and hard about how to fix it."

Brent bristled instinctively at the accusatory tone. "You're assuming whatever's wrong is my fault."

"That's right, I am." Gene folded his arms over his chest. "Claire was terrified for you last night when the bullets started to fly. It's obvious to me that she's in love with you and has acted on her feelings. I'd like to think it's not only lust on your side."

"Gene—"

"I'll trust you not to screw this up."

"I'll do my damnedest not to."

He spoke with a confidence he didn't quite feel. Although he had ammunition to prove to Claire that she'd succeeded in her work, he wasn't sure that would be enough to convince her to stay. She needed a compelling personal reason. She needed him to say that he was open to the possibility of loving her.

For Claire, he could do that. He could let go of the past and embrace a future with her.

If he hadn't already lost her.

THE BREEZE PICKED UP off the lake, sending Claire's list of moving reminders flying. She scrambled to retrieve it, then retreated indoors where she wandered restlessly into the kitchen. She should be making phone calls, making arrangements, getting ready to move on with her life. A life she would continue in Minne-apolis—without Brent.

"Hello, Dr. Lamont," a voice said behind her.

Her heart slammed against her rib cage as she whirled around to find Alec McKenna lounging casually in the kitchen doorway.

A single thought broke free from the chaotic jumble in her mind. "H-how did you find me?"

His lips curved, but the smile didn't reach his eyes. "It took some prompting, but Gene's admin assistant remembered faxing papers for Brent to Weir's Marina. When I showed up there asking for directions, the owner was more than willing to help me out." His gaze moved over her T-shirt, lingering on her breasts in a way that made her feel sick.

"Why are you here?"

"Just tying up some loose ends."

She swallowed. "I thought that's why you were meeting with Gene and the other agents today."

"These are non-FBI loose ends."

She didn't have to feign ignorance. "What are you talking about?"

"Maria Gomez's phone call to you."

How could he know that the nurse had phoned her? Even as the question formed in her mind, she realized the reason didn't matter. All that mattered was the fact that he did. "Forrester's nurse did call me today," she admitted. "She was upset by news reports of his death."

McKenna's eyes narrowed. "And that's all you two talked about?"

"She was the last one to see him the night he escaped. I did my best to calm her down, but she kept repeating that if he hadn't gotten out of Ridsdale, he'd be alive today."

"She called Gene, too," McKenna said, "and left a message with Lisa, which I was lucky enough to intercept. Now how do you suppose she knew his name?"

Was McKenna toying with her? "Maybe she lost my phone number, called the Bureau and got redirected to his line."

He shot her a disgusted look. "Her message said *you* had told her to call. Why would you do that?"

She grasped at a possible explanation. "I thought Gene should know that she was feeling some guilt about Forrester's death, and he might want to ask her more questions about that night."

"Don't lie to me, Claire."

She held his gaze without blinking.

"I think she saw my picture on the news and spilled her guts to you." He added slyly, "Of course, she regrets that decision now."

"What have you done to her?"

"Nothing…yet. Before I left the city, I called to remind her how easily her three-year-old could disappear if she opens her big mouth about me to anybody again."

Relief that the nurse hadn't been harmed was cut short by his next words.

"I'll deal with her…after I've finished with you."

A trickle of sweat ran between her breasts,

and she racked her brain for a way to save herself and the young nurse. "Brent knows that
you coerced Maria Gomez into helping Forrester escape. If something bad happens to her
or me, he'll know you were responsible."

"Brent doesn't know anything and neither
does Gene. I just came from a meeting with
them—"

"I talked to Brent *after* the meeting."

He looked skeptical.

"When we spoke," she continued, "he was
more than halfway here."

Suddenly, she found herself staring at a
wicked-looking ten-inch blade. Backing away,
she made a last-ditch attempt to convince him
not to kill her. "If you leave right now, Brent
won't be able to catch up to you."

"You think so?" His tone was rhetorical.
"Well, it's time you and I left, anyway."

Did he intend to kidnap her? Or was that just

wishful thinking because death was the alternative?

"Where are we going?"

"I rented a speedboat at the marina and docked it not far from here."

"Brent will come after us," she warned, "and he won't stop until he's arrested you."

He turned the knife in his hand, carefully studying the blade. "I'd like to see him try."

A moment ago, his tone had been casual, almost dispassionate. Now both his voice and body language conveyed an eagerness that terrified her. Desperately, she jerked her gaze away from the knife and scanned the kitchen, searching for something she could use to fight him off. In movies, there was always a butcher block of knives close at hand or a heavy cast-iron frying pan on top of the stove. But reality wasn't like that. Reality was a plastic spatula in the dish drainer.

She pressed her fingers against her temple, which had begun to throb.

He gestured toward the hall. "After you."

She walked past him, shoulders slumped, outwardly obedient. But as soon as she pushed open the front door, she leapt off the porch, hitting the ground so hard she bit the inside of her cheek. The taste of blood spurred her on. If she didn't get away, he would shed more of it with that lethal blade he carried.

Sandals slipping on the grass, she darted around the side of the cabin and raced for the trees.

A surprised shout rang out behind her, followed by pounding footsteps and ragged breathing. She pushed herself to run faster. The uneven ground made it risky to lengthen her stride. If she twisted an ankle, he'd be on her in a heartbeat. She had to make it deep into the woods where there might be a place to hide.

She could tell he was closing the distance between them. She dodged left, then scrambled over a fallen log, her lungs burning, her muscles screaming. The denser part of the woods wasn't far off now—

McKenna tackled her.

She sprawled onto the ground with him on top of her, unable to move, unable to breathe. The weight of his body—and her fear—threatened to suffocate her. He would kill her now. Plunge the knife into her and leave her body here, where it would be devoured by scavengers.

He surprised her by grabbing her arm and jerking her to her feet. "That wasn't a smart move." He spat out the words through his teeth, his breath coming in short gasps.

She struggled to catch her own breath,

stumbled twice as she tried to regain her footing. She had lost this chance to escape. It wouldn't be so easy to find another. As he navigated back through the trees without difficulty, she realized he must have scouted out the area earlier.

He propelled her down the hill toward the water. Her footsteps slowed instinctively, until he laid the cold steel of his knife against her throat. She resisted the urge to shiver. "Where are we going?"

"We're taking a ride in the canoe I found in the boathouse."

When they reached it, he opened the door. But instead of going inside, he pushed her ahead of him toward the dock where the canoe was already waiting.

"Why did you leave the door open?"

"Just thought some crumbs would be helpful."

He was setting a scene. When Brent returned to the cabin and didn't find her inside, the open door would automatically lead him to the boathouse and the missing canoe. That's why McKenna hadn't used the knife on her. He wanted to make her death look like an accidental drowning.

She stiffened her spine—no way was she going down without a fight.

The blade fell away from her neck as he pointed to the canoe. "Step in," he ordered. "Sit in the front."

If she dove into the shallow water, McKenna would be on top of her in an instant. Better to wait for another opportunity. She gingerly set one foot, then the other on the wooden slats. The canoe bobbed in the water, giving her an idea. When they reached the middle of the lake, she'd hammer him with a paddle, then dive overboard and escape.

"Let's go," McKenna said.

She dipped the paddle into the water. With her heart pounding and her muscles quivering, it wasn't easy to move them away from the dock.

"Don't get any bright ideas about using that thing as a weapon," he warned. "I still have my knife, and I won't hesitate to kill you."

She didn't doubt him. He pointed to a rocky outcropping in the distance and instructed her to move in that direction.

She was safe as long as she was paddling, so she made a determined effort to delay reaching their destination. Since she hadn't been in a canoe in years, it took little pretense to be awkward with her paddle. Alternating the paddle from side to side, she barely kept the boat going in a straight line.

Fifteen minutes later, they hadn't made much progress.

"Pick up the pace," McKenna ordered.

She swung her paddle out of the water. In her peripheral vision, she saw a flash of wood—the other paddle.

Oh God. She was too slow, her paddle too heavy from the water—

"So long, Dr. Lamont," McKenna said.

A searing pain turned her world black.

Chapter Fifteen

On his way back to the cabin, Brent mentally rehearsed what he was going to say to Claire. He wanted her to understand that his aversion to commitment was a self-defense mechanism. Sylvia's betrayal had cut so deep, he'd relegated his heart to the deep freeze to protect it. Only Claire—with her warm and caring personality—had succeeded in melting away his defenses. Now he was ready to commit unconditionally to their relationship.

His cell phone rang, and he answered it immediately, hoping Claire was on the line.

"Erik Norman here. Sorry it took so long for me to get back to you. I double-checked, and Forrester hasn't been to evidence storage since February eleventh."

That was months before Sharratt had contacted Pete, months before Forrester had known his sweet deal was threatened. Why would the guy have risked stealing Totten's gun back then? It didn't make sense.

"Any chance he could've slipped in unnoticed?" Brent asked.

"It's a secure area. The only way for an agent to gain admittance is to swipe his card, which automatically produces a computer record of his visit."

"Could the records have been tampered with?"

"The Bureau has spent a fortune on security software to prevent that from happening," Norman said.

But if Forrester hadn't been to evidence stor-age since February, how had he acquired that weapon? Maybe he really did have a partner— one who had known about Totten's gun.

"Who else was involved in taking down Hank Totten?" he asked.

The sound of rapid keyboarding was followed by, "Feltz and McKenna."

McKenna.

The agent who had survived the conflagra-tion at Forrester's house with only a bump on the head. The same agent who had shown up unexpectedly at the factory, claimed to see Forrester threaten Brent and shot the man dead.

"See if there's a record of Alec McKenna vis-iting evidence storage in the past six weeks."

As he waited for Norman to run the query, Brent became even more convinced that McKenna had been Forrester's partner in crime.

Which one of them was responsible for killing Sanderson and shooting through Claire's window? Had McKenna passed Totten's gun on to Forrester or had he used it himself?

"Bingo," Norman said. "McKenna was here on May thirtieth."

The day before Sanderson was shot. Too much of a coincidence.

He thanked Norman, disconnected, then called Gene and explained what he'd discovered.

"I'll bring McKenna in for questioning," Gene said grimly.

"Can you ask Lisa about a note she passed to McKenna? He bailed on the meeting soon afterward."

"I'll check into it," Gene promised.

Brent had driven another ten miles when Gene called back.

"Lisa says she gave McKenna a phone

message for me. She remembers Claire had recommended a woman named Maria Gomez contact me. Why does that name sound familiar?"

"Maria Gomez was one of Forrester's nurses at Ridsdale."

"I wonder what she wants."

"As soon as I reach the cabin, I'll ask Claire."

"I had Lisa ring McKenna's place. He's not picking up."

The uneasiness in Brent's gut escalated. McKenna had claimed he was going home when he left the meeting—so where the hell was he?

"Keep trying," he said. "And call me when you get in touch with him."

He increased the Mustang's speed, a sense of urgency growing inside him. McKenna knew from Lisa's note that Claire had talked to

Forrester's nurse. Could he have left the meeting early to try to find Claire? He wouldn't
find her. The only people who knew he and
Claire were staying at the cabin were Gene
and Lisa. Could McKenna have tricked Lisa
into revealing the cabin's location?

He swore as he hit the cabin's speed dial
number on his cell. One ring. Two rings. Three.
Four.

No answer.

He tried not to panic, but his palms were
slick on the steering wheel and his heart ham-
mered against his ribs. Maybe she'd gone for
a swim. Maybe she was sitting outside or had
the radio cranked up. Whatever she was doing,
she'd likely return to the cabin soon because
the weather was turning nasty.

Dark clouds had rolled in, blocking out the
sun. Whenever it rained, the dirt road near
the cabin became treacherous so he pressed

the accelerator to the floor, determined to beat the storm.

The last section of the trip seemed to take an eternity. Finally, he turned off the winding lake road into his laneway. As he caught sight of the cabin, the tension in his shoulders eased. Shutting off the engine, he scooped up the red roses he'd bought for Claire and Gene's envelope of e-mails and headed for the cabin.

The front door stood ajar. He wanted to believe she was just airing out the place, but his instincts warned him otherwise. He vaulted onto the porch, then headed inside, calling her name as he went. The living area, kitchen, both bedrooms and bathroom were all empty. Was she down at the lake?

After leaving the cabin, he set off down the hill, telling himself to calm down. She was fine. He was just on edge because of McKenna.

A minute later, the shoreline came into view. Both Adirondack chairs on the dock were empty. However, the open door of the boathouse suggested she'd been there. When he checked inside, he saw the canoe was missing.

He turned toward the lake and glimpsed something on the water's surface.

A canoe, holding a lone figure. Although the paddler's back was to the shore, he could tell it wasn't Claire.

Oh, God. What had happened to her? His mind reeled at the possibilities.

A cross-current wave rocked the canoe sideways, and he caught sight of an arm trailing over the side. Someone lay face down in the boat, and he suddenly realized where Claire was.

He also got his first look at the paddler's face.

It was Alec McKenna.

BRENT DUCKED inside the boathouse, a murderous rage swelling inside him. He shook it off. Only clear thinking would help him catch McKenna.

Beside him, a shelving unit was piled high with fishing tackle and assorted swim gear. He grabbed a mask and snorkel, then kicked off his shoes and jammed his feet into a pair of fins. On an impulse, he pocketed a sizable fishhook. Wading into the shallow water, he quickly cleared the open end of the boathouse and struck out in a fast crawl.

His stomach churned, and his heartbeat pounded in his ears. He had to reach Claire, had to find out why she lay so still. She couldn't be dead. That belief alone allowed him to stay sane. The canoe hadn't made much headway while he'd been in the boathouse, and he soon discovered why. The lake was choppy because of the approaching storm.

Stroke, breathe.

He tried not to think as he swam, but his mind wouldn't shut off. The thought of losing Claire was unbearable—like fire consuming his flesh, the pain so intense he couldn't endure it. He'd discovered so much in the short time they'd had together. He'd learned to laugh and love, and he did love her—he knew that without a doubt now. Just as he knew a future without her would be barren and joyless.

Stroke, breathe. Stroke, breathe.

After several minutes, he checked on his progress.

The gap between him and the canoe had closed to fifty feet. McKenna seemed oblivious to being followed, but he could look behind him at any moment.

Not wanting to lose the element of surprise, Brent shoved the snorkel into his mouth and submerged his body below the lake's surface.

Then legs and arms pumping like pistons, he propelled himself forward.

When he raised his head, he saw massive rock outcroppings jutting out into the water. The canoe soon disappeared around one of the rocky bends.

He kicked his legs harder, ignoring his aching muscles. He didn't use the snorkel again since the threat of being spotted had ended, and he could make better speed swimming on the surface of the water.

A few minutes passed before he came to the bend. His legs—and brain—stalled at the sight of a sleek, expensive-looking speedboat tethered to a dock less than twenty feet ahead.

What was McKenna up to?

Paddling up to the dock, McKenna carefully stepped onto the wooden platform. Then he tipped the canoe and dumped Claire's limp body into the lake.

Dragging air into his lungs, Brent dove deep, arms and legs straining toward the lake bottom.

A blur of red appeared below him.

Claire had been wearing red today.

The vibrant color had contrasted boldly with her blond hair, and the fabric of the T-shirt had molded softly to her curves. He wished he'd told her how great she looked in that red T-shirt. Dammit, he wanted another chance to tell her. He thrust his hands in front of him but couldn't reach her. Panic bubbled up inside him. She was falling too fast. He couldn't catch her in time. She was going to drown.

No! He could still save her. They could still have the future he wanted for them.

He kicked his legs harder and extended his arms until they felt as if they were pulling free from their socket joints. Come on. Just a few more inches…

His fingertips brushed her shirt. A second later, he was able to latch on it and stop her descent. He felt her hands weakly gripping his forearms. His heart rejoiced that she had regained consciousness, but the relief was fleeting. She had to be perilously close to drowning and so was he. The surface of the water was far above them, and his muscles were flagging from exhaustion.

Lungs bursting from lack of oxygen, he gripped her and with the last of his strength kicked toward the surface. The long shadow of the dock appeared above them.

Three more kicks. Two. One.

Their heads cleared the water in the same instant the speedboat's twin engines roared to life. The noise drowned out Claire's choking and coughing as well as his noisy gasps for air. He hooked a leg around one of the dock's support posts and wrapped his arms around Claire. Although he wanted to savor the moment, he wasn't about to let McKenna get away.

When he eased back to look at her, Claire's lips were moving.

The engines stalled, allowing him to hear what she was trying to tell him.

"McKenna...wants to kill...Maria Gomez," she said.

"I'm going after him."

She bit her lip. "He has a knife."

The engines started up again with an ear-drum-piercing clamor. He swam around to the dock's ladder, discarded his fins and quickly climbed it. The craft was drifting toward open water, drawn by the current. As soon as McKenna shifted the boat into gear, there'd be no hope of catching him.

The speedboat surged forward, and Brent launched himself off the dock. By some miracle, he cleared the engines and came crashing down in the aft section of the boat.

McKenna, kneeling on the driver's seat, jerked his head around at the commotion. His surprised expression changed to one of fury. He yanked the steering wheel hard to the right. Brent tumbled sideways, his right shoulder slamming into the storage compartments. A dark cloud of agony blurred his vision. He must have dislocated his shoulder. He felt lightheaded, but if he passed out, McKenna would make sure he never woke up.

Gritting his teeth, Brent lurched upright. The boat swerved violently again. The sudden movement sent a fresh wave of pain surging through his injured shoulder. Even so, he kept his footing by grabbing hold of the railing with his left hand.

Ahead of him, McKenna was groping for something on the floor near the passenger seat.

Brent let go of the railing and retrieved the fishhook from his pocket. McKenna gave a triumphant cry and began to straighten.

Squeezing between the rear seats, Brent slipped his good arm around McKenna's neck and pressed the point of the fishhook against the other man's jugular vein. "Drop the knife."

McKenna erupted with a stream of profanity.

His shoulder ached so much he didn't know how long he could stay conscious—especially with the boat jarring him mercilessly as it plowed through the waves.

He nicked McKenna's skin next to the vein hard enough to draw blood. "Lose the knife now or I'll kill you."

The knife clattered to the floor of the speedboat.

The pain in his shoulder pulsed like a strobe

light. He had the upper hand, but the situation could reverse in a heartbeat. He gritted his teeth, willing himself to stay conscious. "Take us back to the dock."

He kept the fishhook poised at McKenna's neck as the other man took hold of the wheel, made an 180-degree turn and sped back the way they'd come. Neither he nor McKenna spoke during the trip. He had no inclination to ask questions, partly because he felt so lousy and partly because he wouldn't trust any answers that McKenna gave him, anyway. But he wondered what thoughts preoccupied the other agent. Did McKenna feel guilt or remorse over anything he'd done? Or did he just regret getting caught?

McKenna would be charged and tried for the crimes he'd committed. But no matter what prison term the agent served, it wouldn't bring back Pete.

The speedboat pulled alongside the dock where Claire stood with her arms clasped around her shivering body.

"Sorry to keep you waiting," Brent called out.

She smiled at him. "No problem. I knew you were busy."

As she climbed aboard, the speedboat bumped against the dock.

He bit back a curse. His shoulder felt as if it was on fire, and he was afraid he might black out at any moment. "Grab a mooring line… and tie him up."

She eyed McKenna warily but moved quickly to bind their captive's wrists and ankles.

Brent shoved the other man into the aft section. When he turned back to Claire, he saw her eyes glistening with moisture.

She'd held up amazingly well considering everything she'd been through. But now a combination of shock and relief had her body trembling and tears sliding down her cheeks. He lifted his good arm around her shoulders and hugged her to his side, trying to impart both comfort and warmth. His own body burned from the pain of his injury. Unable to stop himself, he slumped into the driver's seat, pulling her down beside him.

"What's wrong?" Claire asked, her eyes wide with worry.

He tried to reassure her with a smile, but all he could manage was a grimace. "My right shoulder is dislocated."

He closed his eyes, sucked in a shallow breath.

Claire touched his cheek. "Is there anything I can do?"

He forced his eyes open. "Think you can pop my shoulder back in for me?"

She blanched.

"I guess not." As an afterthought, he added, "Pete was squeamish, too, until he got the hang of it."

"I'm sorry he's not here for you," she said in a low voice.

They exchanged a look of silent understanding.

"Can you drive the boat?" Brent asked.

"If you give me some pointers."

"I can do that."

They should have switched seats, but Claire wouldn't let him move. Instead she reached across him to the steering wheel, insisting she had to be on her feet to see over the bow properly.

He was in no shape to argue. All his energy was focused on coping with the pain.

"Where to?" Claire prompted.

He checked the compass on the console,

then looked out at the lake, trying to get his bearings.

He pointed eastward. "The closest marina is five miles that way."

She reached over his shoulder and turned the key in the ignition. Nothing happened. She frowned and tried again.

"You need to set the choke," he told her.

She followed his instructions to start the engine, then looked at him.

"The throttle's over here," he said.

"Oh, yeah."

It was obvious she'd never operated a motorboat before, but with some coaching, she maneuvered the craft away from the dock and set off.

"Watch out for the marina's blue flags," he said, closing his eyes because keeping them open made him dizzy.

He couldn't have done this alone. If Claire

hadn't been here to tie up McKenna and drive the boat, this day would be ending very differently. He and Claire made a great team. If only he could convince her to stay with him.

He came to when Claire's soft voice announced Weir's marina was ahead. He ground his teeth against the pain and opened his eyes to see the floating docks that formed the marina's boundary less than two hundred feet ahead.

Claire cut back on the throttle, steered between the orange buoys that marked the entrance and sought out an empty mooring spot.

"Nice driving," he murmured.

She sank down onto the passenger seat. "How are you feeling now?"

"Like someone's holding a blowtorch to my shoulder."

"I'll get help," she said, rising quickly.

"Good idea, sweetheart. But first—" he gave her a lopsided grin "—kiss me."

She tenderly touched her lips to his.

He needed this woman in his life. Each and every day. Forever.

And as soon as he was sure he wouldn't pass out in midsentence, he would tell her so.

Chapter Sixteen

Claire spent the next couple of hours exhausted and worried.

Gene arrived at the marina with half a dozen other FBI agents to take McKenna into custody, and Brent was hustled away for medical treatment.

She took a seat in the corner and waited while Gene showed two agents where to search for the canoe using the marina's wall map of the lake. He sent the others to look for McKenna's vehicle. Then he turned his attention to her—he wanted to know everything her attacker had said and done from the time he'd arrived at the cabin, yet found it hard to focus on the details. She knew that McKenna would be charged with attempted murder because he'd tried to drown her, but she almost didn't care. All she cared about was Brent.

When they'd taken him away, his face had been gray, his eyes bleary with pain. She needed to see him again, to know that he'd been taken care of. Much more than that, she needed to tell him what was in her heart.

Gene's voice interrupted her thoughts. "Claire, I have to talk with the divers. Can I get you anything before I go? A warm drink? Something to eat?"

She shook her head, drawing the blanket she'd been given tighter around her body. "When do you expect Brent to be here?"

"I'm sure he won't be too much longer," he assured her.

She closed her eyes, relieved to be left alone. The blanket slipped down. Even though she was shivering, she didn't bother to adjust it. Only Brent's arms around her could ease the chill inside her. She tried to think positive thoughts, to remind herself that it was only a dislocated shoulder, and obviously not the first one for him. But she wouldn't be able to relax until she saw for herself that he was okay.

And then what? she wondered. When Brent got back, what would happen next?

She sighed, knowing that the answers to those questions would have to wait until she saw him again.

Then she opened her eyes, and he was there.

Her heart overflowing with relief, she dropped the blanket and ran to his side. She didn't hug him because his right arm was in a sling. Brent still looked tired, but his eyes were no longer glazed with pain, and his lips curved in a smile that was only for her.

"I like you in red," he said, his gaze sliding down to her T-shirt. "And no, I don't have a head injury. I just promised myself I'd tell you that when I got the chance."

She smiled. "How's the shoulder?"

"Back in its proper place," he said. "How are you?"

"Better, now that you're here."

She wanted to reach out to him, to touch him, but the presence of his colleagues made her hesitate.

Just then, Gene strolled over. "When can I expect your written report?"

Brent glanced down at the sling with a grimace. "That's going to take a while, since I'll be typing with one hand."

Gene grinned. "You're lucky you'll be able

to type at all. I doubt McKenna would have hesitated to kill you, too. And by the looks of the knife we confiscated, it would have been quick work."

Claire shivered, remembering the cold metal blade pressed against her throat.

Brent wrapped his good arm around her and hugged her close. "Claire's help was crucial to his capture. After I wrecked my shoulder, she was the one who tied up McKenna, drove the boat here and contacted you."

Claire was surprised—both by his words of praise and the gesture of public affection.

"I've always said she was an asset to the Bureau," Gene said.

The two men exchanged knowing smiles that made Claire wonder what she was missing.

Gene beckoned to a tall, lanky man, who had been pointed out to Claire earlier as the marina owner. "Mac Weir's offered to give you both a ride back to the cabin."

"It's the least I can do for the people who brought my boat back in one piece," the other man said gruffly.

Claire was glad to finally be leaving—and even happier that Brent was coming with her, not staying behind with the rest of the team from the Bureau.

Outside, rain was falling heavily, reducing visibility. The marina owner dropped them at the cabin. She and Brent thanked him for the ride and hurried through the rain to the door. As she stood inside the entry, brushing raindrops from her clothes, Claire caught sight of a long, white box on the coffee table in the living room. "You brought me flowers?" she said, her heart swelling with pleasure at his thoughtful gift.

"Seems like a lifetime ago." With his sling-wrapped arm cupped in his good hand, Brent slowly lowered himself onto the couch and stretched out his long legs.

Claire removed the lid to find a dozen long-stemmed red roses nestled in silver tissue. She inhaled their fragrance, then brushed a finger-tip over a single velvety petal. She swallowed around the sudden lump in her throat. "They're beautiful. Thank you."

"I brought you something else, too," he said. "Something even better than flowers."

"Better than flowers?"

He pointed to an envelope partially obscured by the florist's box.

"What is it?" she asked, bemused.

"Something I think you'll find very enlightening."

She shot him a quizzical look, but he wouldn't say more, so she ripped open the envelope and scanned the first sheet of paper.

By the time she'd finished reading the fifth e-mail, she felt light-headed. The men who had authored these e-mails had praised her so enthusiastically that she kept forgetting to breathe. Prior to this, the most appreciation she'd received was an occasional thanks, muttered in a barely audible voice. But the threat of her dismissal had prompted these intensely private agents to document for the record all the ways that her counseling had helped them.

Over the past few months, her confidence had taken a huge nosedive. Yet here in her hands was proof that she hadn't wasted her efforts, that she had, in fact, made a significant difference to her patients.

Brent was right. This was much better than flowers.

She blinked away the moisture that blurred her vision. "Why didn't Gene tell me?" she asked softly.

"He planned to do that at your next performance review, but then you told him you were quitting the Bureau."

She held the envelope against her chest. Did she really want to leave these agents whose wonderful words of support she would never forget? Did she really want to turn her back on a supervisor who would rally his troops to save her job?

"Gene also mentioned that it was your advice that saved his marriage."

She curled up next to Brent on the couch. "He really said that?"

"I'll take a polygraph if you want," he said solemnly.

She smiled. "That won't be necessary."

He reached for her hand. "I haven't thanked you properly for helping me. In light of all your other accolades, I guess one more hardly matters, but I wanted you to know."

"What you think matters a great deal to me."

He gazed at her in silence for a long time. Then, just as she sensed he was about to speak, his cell phone rang. He made no move to answer it.

"It might be important," she pointed out.

"This is important," he said.

She nodded. "And we'll finish it after your call."

He released her hand and pulled out his cell phone.

While he spoke in a low voice, her thoughts wandered. Starting a new job had lost its appeal now that she felt validated in her current position. And tonight's short separation from Brent had shown her how much she wanted to be with him. Because she loved him.

She was going to tell him how she felt, confident they had a chance at a real relationship.

As for Balanced Life Consulting Group, they would just have to find somebody else to teach stress-management courses to executives.

Brent set down his cell phone. "That was Gene," he told her. "They found McKenna's car and have already torn it apart. Hidden inside the passenger seat, they found a gun that looks like the one that was used to kill Pete and shoot through your front window."

She shuddered. "I'm surprised McKenna didn't bring it when he came to the cabin. It would've been simpler—and quicker—than renting a speedboat and paddling to that dock."

"I think he wanted Forrester to take the blame for what happened before today. So your death had to look accidental—as if you'd paddled to the dock, then slipped and hit your head as you stepped out of the canoe."

"I hope he has a long time in prison to

think about everything he's done," she said vehemently.

"He will. I'm sure the gun is only the first piece of evidence we'll find. He killed Pete and Harris—no one's going to let him get away with any of it."

"Pete would approve of everything you've done to bring McKenna to justice."

"I think so, too," Brent agreed. "But when I went after McKenna today, I wasn't thinking of Pete. I was only thinking of you. I wanted to kill him for trying to hurt you."

"You saved my life today."

He smiled. "And you saved mine."

Beyond the living-room windows, lightning streaked toward the lake in a jagged flash of brilliance, and the wind whipped the trees.

"Do you remember the night Gene sent you to get me—after Forrester had escaped from Ridsdale?"

He rubbed his nose. "How could I forget?"

She smiled. "There was a storm that night, too." But the terror she'd felt was gone. She was with Brent, safe and secure in his arms.

"I hope we'll see many more together," Brent said.

She glanced up at him and held her breath, almost afraid to hope.

He looked back at her, his eyes filled with an emotion she hadn't seen in them before.

"I think you know," he continued, "that I've never had a problem putting my life on the line. But putting my heart on the line? That's an entirely different story. No serious relationships means no way to get hurt, right?"

His mouth twisted in a grimace. "I don't want to play it safe by limiting myself to work—and nothing else—anymore."

"What do you want?" Claire asked.

"I want you." He stroked her cheek with a

gentle finger. "My heart nearly stopped when I saw McKenna overturn that canoe. In that moment, I finally realized how much I loved you. I'd have known it sooner if I hadn't been blinded by stubbornness, but nearly losing you made my feelings crystal clear. I love you, Claire, and I don't ever want to let you go."

Her heart expanded until she could feel it pressing against her ribs. "I love you, too, Brent. So much."

At last, he kissed her. He kissed her deeply, thoroughly, endlessly until her head was spinning. As always, she tasted passion on his lips, but this time there was a tenderness that warmed her soul.

She drew back to catch her breath. "Does this mean I can look forward to something more than a few dates in our future?"

"Definitely more than a few dates," he

promised. "Maybe even marriage and children—if that's still what you want."

She was too overwhelmed to speak.

He leaned his forehead against hers. "I want to make a life with you, Claire. I want us to share our best and worst moments and be together always." He drew back and searched her eyes, his gaze reflecting the love his words had just expressed. "My gut tells me we can make that happen."

She gave him a tremulous smile. "My heart agrees."

"What about the Bureau?"

She realized she hadn't told him she'd changed her mind about leaving. Everything had happened so fast, she hadn't had a chance. "Do you think Gene will take me back?"

"You know he will. But is that what you really want? Because if it's not, I could ask for a transfer—"

She stopped him with a hand against his lips. "I appreciate your offer, but those e-mails—along with everything else that's happened in the past twenty-four hours—have given me a whole new perspective."

"I'm glad."

She wrapped her arms around his waist. "How long before your shoulder heals?"

He nuzzled her earlobe. "Doctor said that depends on how much I restrict my activity."

"What does that mean exactly?"

"I have no idea." He shifted her suddenly so that she sprawled on top of him. "But I do know how resourceful you can be in times of need."

"I need you," she whispered.

He brushed several strands of hair back from her face. "The feeling's mutual, sweetheart."

She slid her hands over the part of his chest not covered by his sling. "I don't want to hurt you."

"I'm willing to risk it if you are."

She caressed his sculpted cheeks and looked deep into his eyes. "Loving you is no risk at all."

"I was just thinking the same thing," he said sincerely.

"Then it's official. We belong together—"

"—in every way possible." Easing down the neckline of her shirt, he kissed the sensitive skin he'd uncovered. Then he used his teeth and tongue and hands to explore the rest of her—in every way possible.

As much as his touch excited her, she was even more thrilled by the love she saw in his eyes. They'd both almost died today and joining their bodies together now felt natural and right. It was more than making love.

It was a celebration of life.

* * * * *

WEB_M&B_RTL3 LP

Discover Pure Reading Pleasure with

Visit the Mills & Boon website for all the latest in romance

🌹 **Buy** all the latest releases, backlist and eBooks

🌹 **Find out** more about our authors and their books

🌹 **Join** our community and chat to authors and other readers

🌹 **Free** online reads from your favourite authors

🌹 **Win** with our fantastic online competitions

🌹 **Sign** up for our free monthly eNewsletter

🌹 **Tell us** what you think by signing up to our reader panel

🌹 **Rate** and review books with our star system

www.millsandboon.co.uk

 Follow us at twitter.com/millsandboonuk

 Become a fan at facebook.com/romancehq